1

LET'S GET RADIOACTIVE!

I'm lying on a steel table, all too aware of the giant ray gun pointed in my direction. It looks like one of those room-sized five-ton laser things supervillains use in movies. The kind they threaten to destroy the planet with.

"What music're you into, Ross?"

I'm pretty sure the radiation tech is just trying to distract me as he bolts me down. A hard-plastic-mesh mask over my neck and head holds me still—they molded it to my face yesterday—and the tech struggles to click it onto the table. He scrunches his nose, pushing.

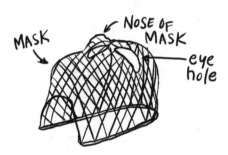

MASK

NOSE OF MASK

eye hole

"Oh . . . anything. Whatever," I mumble through my teeth. The hardened mask doesn't let my chin move much.

The headpiece locks in, and the tech—Frank—gives my shoulder a bump with his fist. "C'mon, man. If you're gonna lie here for half an hour, you need some tunes. I've got all kinds. Name something you like. There are no wrong answers."

I scan my brain. "You could . . . Can you just . . . KZAQ?"

Frank stops and doubles over at the waist like he's been gut-punched. He hangs there, talking to the floor.

"Okay . . . No wrong answers but that one." He straightens up and winces at me. "Seriously? You like that Top Forty garbage?"

"It's . . . what my parents have on all the time . . ."

So dorky. I try to look away casually, but my head won't budge.

Frank stares before letting out an exaggerated sigh.

"*Fine*. But tomorrow, tell me what *you* like. Not what Mom and Dad like." He walks over and fiddles with an old-timey boom box on a high wall shelf, next to a teetering stack of CDs and cassette tapes.

Seriously? There must be a gazillion dollars worth of equipment in here, and they can't afford an MP3 player? I notice a bit of tattoo peeking out from the arm of Frank's scrubs. A lizard tail, maybe? Or a tentacle?

WINK

ROB HARRELL

HOT
KEY
BOOKS

For Amber

First published in Great Britain in 2020 by
HOT KEY BOOKS
4th Floor, Victoria House, Bloomsbury Square, London WC1B 4DA
Owned by Bonnier Books
Sveavägen 56, Stockholm, Sweden
www.hotkeybooks.com

A CIP catalogue record for this book is available from the British Library.

ISBN: 978-1-4714-0914-1
Also available as an ebook

3

Design by Jason Henry • Text set in Aptifer Slab LT Pro
Printed and bound in Great Britain by Clays Ltd, Elcograf S.p.A.

Hot Key Books is an imprint of Bonnier Books UK
www.bonnierbooks.co.uk

Beyoncé fills the room, and suddenly Frank is all business. "I know we went over this yesterday, but let's review."

He wraps his arms around his clipboard and begins, like he's done this a thousand times.

"The gurney you're on is going to lift you up and move you into place. The treatment takes twenty-five minutes or so. Keep your limbs and naughty bits inside the ride at all times. Do not throw things at the radiation techs. Do not FEED the radiation techs. Do not waggle your legs around like a synchronized swimmer. Do not pass Go. Do not hum the Goo Goo Dolls, as I DESPISE the Goo Goo Dolls."

Frank steps aside to let another tech—Callie, I think—reach in and mold some blue clay over the bridge of my nose. She smiles at me and tells me it's to protect my "good" eye from the beam. Then she pats my chest. I hope I don't look as nervous as I feel, 'cause I feel like a rabbit in a trap. My face is hot.

"Okay. Now for the important part." Frank is back. "When I tell you, you're gonna stare at the red X above you. The one we made over there by the big zapper yesterday. You'll see it when the machine slides you over."

The mask prevents much of a nod, but he seems to catch it. "Don't move your eye off of that X, or your eye'll explode into a million pieces like the Death Star, m'kay?"

I let out a little grunt.

Frank puts his hand on my arm. "I'm kidding, Ross. I mean . . . kind of. Don't look away from the X. Your eye won't explode, but we're dealing with your vision. Important stuff. So keep your eye on the X, or it could . . . Just keep your eye on the X, and you'll be fine."

Callie steps back in with a U-shaped attachment that looks like part of a kid's car seat. She fits it over my face and helps me slip the molded mouthpiece into my mouth. My teeth lock into it when I bite down, and she snaps the ends of the U to the table. *Ka-chunk.* The table is attached to a huge mechanical arm, like something out of *Star Trek.*

My nose itches. I couldn't move my head if I had to, and something about that makes me all squirmy inside. I feel like a bug on a dissecting table.

Frank and Callie look down at me. "You good?" Callie squeezes one of my sock-covered toes. "Need a blanket?"

"Nuh, I'n goo."

"Okay." She tucks a lock of hair behind her ear and gives me a friendly smile. Everybody smiles a lot here, probably because they can tell I'm freaking out. "We'll be right around the corner. You'll do great."

Frank winks. "No sweat. You'll see."

They walk off to my left, but I can't turn my head to follow them. The lights dim slowly as Gwen Stefani starts singing about bananas.

I'll admit it. It's a little freaky being the only one in here with all this machinery. All this . . . *stuff*.

I close my eyes and let out a long breath. It shudders as it slowly comes out, which somehow takes my nerves up another notch.

"All right." Frank's voice squawks through a tinny speaker. "We're gonna get started, Ross. Just relax and keep your eye on the red X. You're about to go for a ride."

After a few seconds of silence, there are loud bangs and a revving sound. The entire room full of heavy machinery comes to life with beeping and whirring and what might be big fans powering up. Maybe things heat up when the radiation gets going? I have no idea.

Then the gurney shudders, and I begin to rise.

Frank comes through the speaker again.

"Houston, we have liftoff."

2

PROTONAPALOOZA

My vocabulary of scientific terms has grown by leaps and bounds in the last few months.

Biopsy. Malignant. Mucoepidermoid. Carcinoma. Lacrimal gland. Resection. Triangulation. Proton radiotherapy. I may be in seventh grade, but I ought to be qualified for med school by the end of this.

The hardest part of the treatment is keeping my eye focused in the center of that red X. The whole thing makes me incredibly nervous. If someone tells you not to think about a purple elephant, it's suddenly the only thing you can think about.

The harder I try to keep my eye still, the more it wants to slide off of the X. And my eye isn't the only thing drifting. My brain keeps taking me back to the day this all started . . .

So, there have been a few really Bad Days through this whole thing. Capital *B*, capital *D*. The first one was a few months ago. Mid-July. Right smack in the middle of what was supposed to be an awesome, relaxing summer.

The buildup to Bad Day #1 started when I'd been lying upside down in a chair reading *To Kill a Mockingbird*. It was a summer reading assignment, and while I'm strongly against summer schoolwork, I had to admit it was a pretty good book. I got up and walked into the kitchen, and my dad's eyes got wide.

"Whoa! What happened there?"

I had no idea what he was talking about, so I opened the pantry door, searching for food. "What happened where?"

He came over and carefully touched the area above my eye. "Does that hurt?"

"Does what hurt?" I stepped into the hallway and looked in the mirror.

My eyelid was all puffed out—it looked like a bullfrog's neck when they blow their necks up.

"Whoa! That is nasty!" I poked at it. It was pretty gross, like it was full of fluid. We talked about whether I'd been bitten by something (no) or gotten hit by something (no)—and decided to ice it.

It went down over the next half hour, so we forgot about it.

Until the next day—Sunday—when I woke up late with another case of Frog Eye. We iced it again. Then, Monday morning, my dad took one look at me and called out of work—which is a super big deal—and we drove to see some eye specialist, Dr. Sheffler.

Dr. Sheffler told me I needed a "cat scan."

Turns out that's lingo for a procedure called a CT scan, but for a little while I was picturing a doctor waving a cat over me.

Thirty minutes later, I was in an ancient building near the hospital. I found myself wearing a hospital gown—the dumbest, most butt-revealing garment ever designed—padding down a cold hallway in little brown socks with treads on the bottom. They put me on a steel bed, my feet sticking through a giant mechanical donut, and at this point I started getting genuinely nervous—and kind of wishing my dad hadn't stayed in the waiting room.

A truly enormous male nurse—he looked like he should play for the Colts—came in and put an IV in my arm (needle one out of three billion if I'm counting).

He warned me, "Ross, when I inject this, it might feel like you're peeing your pants."

It made me laugh—until a few minutes later when he squirted the contrast dye into the IV line and I got all warm and felt EXACTLY LIKE I WAS PEEING MY PANTS!

Even though I WASN'T PEEING! OR WEARING PANTS!

So weird. It couldn't have felt MORE like I was peeing if I'd actually just let go and whizzed myself.

Sorry.

I digress.

Afterward, Dad and I went to grab an early sub at Dagwood's, as they have awesome milkshakes and their sandwiches are the best thing ever put between two slices of bread.

Dr. Sheffler had told us we'd probably get the results

in two or three days, so it was pretty far from my mind as my dad parked out front. I was busy considering the wide array of delicious sandwich options I'd soon have.

Then my dad's phone rang. He pulled it out, looked at the screen, and frowned. My dad was looking over at me when he answered.

"Hello?"

I only heard my dad's side of the conversation.

"Yes, it is."

"Wait. You did?"

"Okay."

"Right now?"

"All right."

"Absolutely. We'll be there in five minutes."

He hung up and slid the phone all the way into the pocket of his jeans before he said anything. "That was, uh . . . Dr. Sheffler. He has your scans. Wants to see us now."

"Is that bad?"

"Nah . . ." He started the car. "I don't think so." He was trying to sound casual, but his face had gone kind of slack. "Let's just swing over there and . . . you know, we'll grab . . . we'll do Dagwood's afterward."

I peppered him with questions, but he assured me the doctor hadn't told him anything.

Then he was just quiet, which wasn't like him. I'd have killed for a knock-knock or a dad joke right about then.

"So," Dr. Sheffler said, when we were back in his office. He used his foot to hook a rolling stool over and sat down in front of us. He set down the file he'd been holding and leaned in, his elbows on his knees like a basketball coach in a huddle. I felt my dad tense up beside me. I cracked a few knuckles.

"Thank you for coming so quickly," Dr. Sheffler continued, speaking carefully. "Let's not beat around the bush. The scan picked up something. A mass, above your right eye." He looked right at me, his mouth squeezed in a tight line—it was a look that somehow said *I'm sorry I have to tell you this* and *This is serious business that we need to discuss like adults* at the same time.

"Really?"

I'll never forget the way my dad said it. *Ree. A. Lee?* Like he'd just found out dragons exist, or that day is night.

That's honestly the last thing I remember clearly.

I mean, I didn't pass out or anything, but they kept talking while my body and head went kind of fuzzy.

I heard bits and pieces.

". . . tumor? No way to know yet . . ."

". . . needle biopsy as soon as we can . . ."

". . . could be benign, but let's . . ."

". . . in the lacrimal gland above the right . . ."

". . . size of a gumball . . ."

". . . not time to panic yet . . ."

Then all of a sudden, we were at the somber shaking-of-hands and thank-you part. They'd schedule this and that and call us.

And then we were outside. Sitting on the couple of steps outside the front door.

My dad pulled me into him and rubbed the top of my head. Gave it a casual kiss that seemed anything but casual.

"It's all gonna be fine, Ross. Okay? The dumb thing is most likely benign, y'know?"

We sat there for a while, him rubbing my shoulder. I kept thinking, *How serious is this?*

I remembered when my mom went through this— even though I was only four when she did—that "benign" was the good kind of tumor. Or, not good, but not necessarily dangerous. "Malignant" was the bad kind: Cancer. The *Big C.*

But—what now? Was I supposed to cry? Should I wail

and throw myself down on the ground? It would have been helpful if Dr. Sheffler had given me a chart, from one to ten, circled the six and said, *This right here is how much you should freak out at this point.*

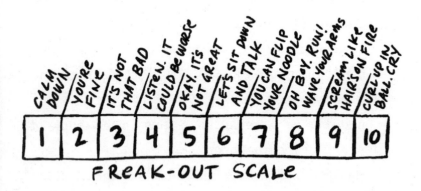

FREAK-OUT SCALE

While I sat on the office steps, my dad went a few paces down the walk to call my stepmom, Linda. Then he called my grandmother (Gammy) in St. Louis, who sniffled and called me Rossy about a thousand times when I got on the phone.

I thought about texting my friends Abby and Isaac, but I couldn't yet. I had no idea what I'd say.

Later, when we got home, Linda set something yellow out for dinner that I poked at but didn't eat.

I remember sitting in the basement playing *Annihilation: Moon* until my thumbs ached.

Eventually, the day got dark and ran out the way

even the worst days do. I went to bed but couldn't sleep, so I just lay there watching headlights slide across my ceiling to the sound of my dad and Linda low-talking in the next room.

All I felt was numb.

3

BACK TO REALITY

My entire body jerks, and my heart starts pounding. That big X is staring down at me, and the mesh mask has me trapped. Did I start to fall asleep? That's a super scary thought, given the whole don't-let-your-eye-drift, exploding-eyeball thing. I blame it on the slow song that was playing at the time. Frank may have a point about me needing better radiation jams.

Then, suddenly, it's over, and Frank and Callie are back in the room unhooking me. Unmouthpiecing. Unmasking. Frank sticks out a hand and helps me sit up.

"You did pretty good for a first-timer. In three more days, you'll be a pro. And by the end of your eight weeks, you'll be stealing my job." He squints like he's inspecting me. Judging me. "Right? I can see it in your eyes."

He looks over at Callie. "He looks shifty, doesn't he?

It's the beady eyes. We need to watch our backs." Callie is looking at something on her clipboard. She gives me a quick roll of her eyes.

As I hop down, Frank leans in and stage-whispers, "Don't mind Callie. She has an *enormous* crush on me, the poor thing."

Callie blurt-laughs and walks away. "See you tomorrow, Ross!"

I put on my shoes and grab my backpack from a locker by the door.

We pass Dr. Throckton's office on the way out. He's known to my family by the superhero-like name "the Man with All the Answers"—and he's the doctor in charge of my radiation. He's behind his desk, his hair sticking up comically, like he's been running his hands through it. Both feet are propped up on his desk, and he has his phone to his ear—but when he sees me, his eyes light up. He covers the mouthpiece and yell-whispers to me.

"How'd it go?"

"Good, I guess?" I answer. He pinches the phone between his shoulder and cheek and gives me two thumbs-ups. There's a blue ink stain on one of them.

Frank walks me down the hall to the waiting room,

asking if middle school is as unbearable as he remembers.

"It's all right." I shrug as we go through the electric double doors, into the waiting room.

As waiting rooms go, this one is pretty swanky. There are a bunch of comfortable couches and chairs arranged around several big aquariums. Halloween decorations are out, since it's only a few days away. There's even a complimentary drink station, with coffee and a fridge full of soft drinks and little water bottles.

I don't see my stepmom. My guess is Linda ran to Starbucks for more iced green tea. She's always running out for green tea.

VENTi,
HALF-ICE
ONe
SPLeNDA

An old guy sits beside one of the aquariums, sipping a cup of coffee. He lifts the cup in salute.

Frank steers me over. "Ross, I want you to meet someone. Or to be more accurate, warn you to stay far, far away from him."

We stop in front of the guy. "Jerry, this is Ross. He just had his first treatment." Then he addresses me. "Ross, this here is the oldest, crankiest man ever to stalk the planet."

Jerry laughs—a wheezy, good-natured laugh—as he struggles up to the front of his seat. I shake his enormous hand. It feels like it's made out of limestone.

"They stuck you with Frank, huh? I'd say it could be worse, but I'm not sure how." Then his bushy eyebrows go up. "Go okay in there?"

"I think so. I guess?" I look away at the fish in the tank beside him. Why am I always so awkward?

"There ya go. Just lay back and let these guys do the hard stuff, right?" Jerry has a rough, deep voice—it reminds me of gravel in a blender. He leans back, and I notice the blue mesh band at the bend of his arm where he's had blood drawn. I've gotten annoyingly familiar with blood draws. I can tell you where my juiciest vein is, which is just weird.

Frank scans the waiting room. "Where's your mom, Ross?"

"Stepmom."

"Stepmom. Did she skip out on you? Flee the country?"

"Probably." I sit on the edge of a couch. I know how to wait. That's what phones are for.

"Well . . . if you're still here in three hours, I'll give you a ride. Least I can do."

Jerry shakes his head. "Oh, good Lord. Don't take that ride. They'll let anybody have a license these days."

Frank starts to walk away. "Keep trying, Jerry. You'll say something funny one of these days." Then he spins around to walk backward, pointing at me with both fingers like guns.

"Forty-four zaps to go, Ross. But, seriously. Tomorrow. I want suggestions for REAL music. Or I start playing you some of mine." He jams his backside into the doors and is gone.

Jerry studies me, deadly serious. "Do it. Bring music, or he's likely to play his band's CD. You've suffered enough."

"He's in a band?"

He blows on his coffee. "In the loosest sense of the

word." Then he grabs a magazine, so I guess I can take out my phone without looking too rude. I text Abby.

> Zap 1 in the books.

She texts back immediately.

> Was it bad? Are you a radiated mutant like Godzilla now?

> Not really, but I can shoot laser beams out of my butt.

> OOH! So jealous. Seriously, though. Did it hurt?

> Nope.

> Aces.

Abby had asked to come today, but I told her I didn't want to make a big deal out of it. She pressed, but I insisted she not come. If she'd come, there would've been hugs and high fives, and it would have been a Big Deal, and I feel like if I give this thing as little energy as I can, it'll just . . . fade away.

I think Abby understood. Eventually.

The front doors fly open, and my stepmom stalks in on a cloud of cool air and caffeine. "Ross! You're out! I'm so sorry. I needed a jolt, so I hopped over to Bucky's and thought I'd get back before you were out! How was Day One?"

One of the more annoying things about Linda is her insistence on calling Starbucks Bucky's. It gives me chills.

She stops in front of me and looks over at Jerry. "Hello."

I start to get up. "That's Jerry."

Jerry starts the process of standing up to shake her hand. "That's me. I'm Jerry Thompson . . ."

Linda flaps her hands at him. "Oh, no need to get up. We have to get going. It's nice to meet you, Jerry. I'm Linda." They shake hands quickly, and she turns to me. "You ready? I need to get you home. I have about two million things I need to do." She turns to Jerry and rolls her eyes. "Real estate."

Jerry smiles. "Ah, yes. Big doings." Then he kicks my foot lightly with one of his Velcro orthopedic shoes. "Nice meeting you, Ross. I'll see you around. I'm glad your Day One went well."

I stand up and pocket my phone. "Nice meeting you too. What day of your treatment are you on?"

"This round? Day Thirty-six. But who's counting?"

■ ■ ■

Linda's phone starts chirping as soon as we're in her Grand Cherokee, and we ride home to the sounds of Linda talking up a beautiful little three bedroom/two bath not too far from the lake. It apparently has amazing light and the most adorable breakfast nook.

I text Isaac, not really expecting him to text back. He hasn't been around much lately. Like. Not at all.

> Hey. What's up? I just got radiated like the Hulk.

I sit there watching my screen, and I'm kind of surprised when the three dots start up. He's texting back for once?

The three dots flash, and flash and flash . . . And then they go away. I'm a little embarrassed to admit it, but my heart sinks. What's going on with him? I wait, staring, for the dots to start again, but they don't.

Eventually I cram my phone back in my pocket. The rest of the way, I just space and stare out the window. I've been getting pretty good at that lately.

At home, I go straight upstairs. I drop my pack and head to the mirror in my bathroom. There's no visible mark where the beam went in by my temple. Weird.

But looking in the mirror brings up some bad memories, seeing my scar and my closed, squinty, permanently winking eye. The biopsy. The diagnosis. The surgery. I try to keep that kind of looking to a minimum, so I don't get all wigged out.

Eventually I go in and flop facedown on my bed. My phone starts buzzing in my pocket, but I'm asleep before you can say "proton radiation therapy."

I have a dream where I'm a french fry in a basket, getting lowered again and again into thick boiling oil. It sounds really dumb, but it's completely terrifying.

When I wake up, my room is mostly dark, and my dad is sitting next to me on the bed, his hand on my back. "Hey, Ross. You awake?"

I grunt yes, kind of.

"How'd it go? I want all the details."

I roll over slowly, half awake. His hair is messed up on one side, and he's loosened his tie. He needs a shave.

"Wow," I say. "You look awful."

He laughs and rubs his face with both hands. "Ha. Yeah. It was a day. And all I wanted was to be there with you." He's a trial lawyer, and he's in the middle of some big megacase. It's about some huge insurance settlement or something.

He lets out a long sigh, like he's been holding his breath for days. "So, spill. Gimme the dirt. Start at the beginning and don't leave anything out."

So I slide back against my headboard, he settles back beside me, and I tell him.

4

SCHOOL FUN. YAY.

When I get to school the next morning, Abby is less than thrilled with me—I fell asleep and missed a bunch of texts from her. We drop her viola off in the band room, and as we make our way down the hallway— past a kid dumping crazy amounts of spit out of his trumpet—she lets me hear about it.

"You forget how to return a freakin' text? I thought maybe they aimed wrong and your brains fizzled out after you got home." She's digging through her backpack trying to find something. ChapStick, most likely.

She's the only person who jokes with me about my "situation"—she's done it through most of this whole ordeal—and I literally could not appreciate it more. It makes me feel like something in the world is normal.

I mean, don't get me wrong. It'd be weird if everybody else joked about it.

But it's Abby.

Abby Peterson has been my best friend since the third day of first grade, when I choked on some milk and a Flintstones gummy vitamin shot out of my nose—a Dino, I think. She laughed so hard she almost threw up—and a forever bond was formed.

Around fourth grade, we welcomed the eternal goof Isaac Nalibotsky into our friend group—it was an easy fit—but he's been acting weird lately. He's just vanished, as far as hanging out with us is concerned. He'd normally be making this walk with us, and it's still bizarre that he isn't.

"I just really didn't feel like talking," I said. "Or texting. Or lifting my head off the pillow. Did you do the Language Arts homework? I totally ignored it."

"Pssh. I think Ms. Bayer'll let it slide. You only have, like, the ultimate excuse ever. 'Oh, I'm terribly sorry, but I had a beam of pure energy shot into my head yesterday.'" She slathers on enough lip balm for three people. "But how was it? Was the beam hot?"

We stop at my locker so I can grab my math textbook. "It was . . . It didn't feel like anything. I just have to lie there for a while, and then I'm done. It's pretty weird."

Abby stares at me for a few seconds, thinking. "Yeah, that isn't gonna cut it. When people ask, you need to drama it up a bit—for them if not for you."

"Okay. Right." I shut my locker with a bang. I notice a couple of girls watching us. I'm pretty sure they're sixth grade. "Maybe I say I could smell burning flesh. Or I could hear my eye sizzling like bacon."

"You joke, but I wouldn't stop there." Abby puts an elastic thingy between her lips, gathering her wavy orange hair into a ponytail. Puts her headband in her backpack. "You can milk this whole laser beam sci-fi thing as far as you wanna go, friend. You're school-famous."

Such an Abby thing to say. If there's one thing Abby enjoys, it's standing out. Which is good, as her tangerine-colored hair can be seen from space. Add to that an eccentric sense of fashion—some would just call it insane—and Abby is someone you can't miss. But her nutso style helps me out. I'm all but invisible standing next to her.

Actually, I *used* to be invisible. I could walk through a crowded library and escape completely unnoticed. Unscathed. Hardly anybody talked to me, and I lived peacefully under the radar like a stealth bomber in a hoodie. I never realized it before, but it was kind of great.

Then, y'know . . . cancer.

Gone were my big plans to sneak my way through seventh grade with my non-noteworthy B average, unnoticed by teachers and students alike. Now I can't walk the length of a hallway without someone studying me to see if I look sick. Or just staring. Or even worse, they ask how I'm feeling.

One kid came up to me and in hushed tones asked if I was dying. He was in sixth grade, so I think he was honestly just unsure what to say. Another kid, an eighth grader named Billy Herrold, just came up and nodded—then told me his uncle died of cancer.

I wasn't really sure what to do with that info, so I just gave him a half smile and said, "That's too bad." He walked away like he was proud he'd opened up to the sick kid, but I had a worried knot in my stomach for two periods after that.

I think those kids are trying to be nice—or at least act nice—but I'd give my right eye to be Anonymous Kid again, which is a super stupid thing to say, 'cause my right eye is where I had my tumor.

One of my worst cancer moments happened when the school did something that was—again—supposed to be nice. Since my surgery happened later in the summer, I missed the first week of school, recovering. On my first day back, I found a *huge* card signed by the teachers and everyone in my class.

They'd written messages all over it. *Get better! Sorry you're sick!* and the always helpful *Cheer up!*

I was horrified. It had been a few weeks since the surgery, and except for some yellowing bruises, I looked relatively okay. But that card said, *Forget sneaking back into school like Mr. Normal.* It was like someone had hung a big lit-up sign over my head announcing what had happened. *Sick Kid right here!*

■ ■ ■

When I get to class, Ms. Bayer appears next to my desk.

"How are you doing, Ross? You started your treatment yesterday, right?"

I feel a few sets of eyes on us. "Yeah. I'm okay."

She settles into the desk across the aisle and gives me a concerned look. A mass of bracelets clack and jangle as she puts a reassuring hand on my arm. People like to touch your arm reassuringly when you're sick, I've noticed.

"Okay. Well, let me know if you need anything, or if the homework gets on top of you."

I nod and think of Abby saying I have the Ultimate Excuse.

"I . . . um . . . I was pretty tired when I got home. I didn't get the worksheets done, but I . . ."

Ms. Bayer smiles and leans in like she has a secret, wafting thick perfume. "Don't you worry. Get them in as soon as you feel up to it, okay?" Her eyebrows go up so far, she looks like a cartoon. "Just keep talking with me, all right? Keep me in the loop." She stands up and walks back to the front of the room.

I blink, a little stunned. Bayer is one of the strictest teachers in the school.

What magic is this?

I'm wondering how far I can take this new power of

mine when Sarah Kennedy floats in and the room brightens like somebody upped the wattage in all the bulbs.

She heads to her desk, directly in front of me. Awkward energy floods my body as I busy myself getting out some pens and paper for notes. I have to actually work at looking casual, even though I know she isn't looking remotely in my direction.

Then she looks.

"Hey."

I look behind me to make sure she isn't talking to someone else. She isn't. "Yeah?" All noise has dropped out of the room except for a high ringing in my ears.

"I'm out of paper. Could I borrow a few sheets?"

She smiles her ridiculously bright smile, and I feel my throat tighten. Sarah Kennedy has this effect on me. She has this effect on a *lot* of people in my school, if I'm being honest. I know there's nothing terribly enlightened about going all gooey over a girl I barely know, but . . . well . . . blame puberty.

Sarah isn't just popular and good-looking and super amazingly smart. A couple of years ago I saw her at the park with her older brothers . . . and she was skateboarding. *Skateboarding!* And she was good at it! It was the coolest thing I've ever seen. It was like seeing the Queen of England hop a curb.

It's burned in my memory forever. I even thought about taking up skateboarding myself. Then I borrowed Isaac's and just about killed myself and decided that wasn't happening. Coordination and I are not friends.

"Mm-hm. Sure." I pull out a couple of sheets of paper, but my fine motor skills have fled the building. My hand chooses to crumple them as they come out, so I shove them in my backpack and pretend it didn't happen. I go into my folder for a few more and hold them out for her.

Then comes a deep voice to my right. "So, what? You got superpowers 'n' crap now?"

I turn slowly.

It's Jimmy Jenkins.

"Nope," I say. "No superpowers. Not yet."

Jimmy is the biggest kid in our year. Definitely the sketchiest. I've heard stories—about him being mean or crazy or both—and frankly, it freaks me out that I have to sit by him. An encounter with Jimmy is like handling a grizzly bear. One wrong word can result in him getting angry, and you don't want him angry.

I heard, in fifth grade, he gave a kid a noogie so bad the kid went to the hospital. And last year he supposedly roughed up a high school junior over a football bet or something.

Jimmy's tongue expertly adjusts an enormous wad of gum—grape Big League Chew, most likely—around his mouth as he considers this. He's always chomping on an enormous ball of the stuff. It's gross. His mouth gets all wet when he chews it, and then he ends up sticking those big blobs wherever he feels like when he's done. I've stepped or sat in a couple of Jimmy Wads, as they're known around the school.

To make it even grosser—sorry—he carries this little juice bottle around with him and spits in it. I don't know if he thinks it's like he's chewing tobacco or if he has some kind of saliva problem, but it's literally the nastiest thing ever. I've had nightmares about it.

"Sucks for you. Did that cancer beam make ya crap your pants or anything?"

All of my blood has gone to my ears, and I can feel Sarah watching the exchange.

"No. Nope." My voice cracks. "None of . . . that."

"Yeah? How 'bout yer piss. Does it glow in the dark? I heard that happens."

This is like threading a needle. Don't poke the bear, but maintain dignity in front of Sarah.

"Not . . . not that I've noticed."

"Mm. Too bad." Jimmy grunts and starts chewing again. He shifts his oversized bulk to face front again. His interest in me has run its course.

Sarah is still looking back, holding the paper. Is she looking at my scar? My squinty eye? I tip my head away from her just in case.

"Well. Thanks for this. I used all my paper on . . ." She lifts up a thick stack of flyers and hands me one. "For the Christmas talent show. It's in December. End of the semester. Maybe you could do some of your drawings or characters onstage or something?"

I take the flyer, trying to imagine how that would go—me doodling onstage while students yawn and die from boredom in the front row.

My cheeks flush deep red at the thought.

I'm a doodler, not an artist. Huge difference. My mom was an artist. An illustrator, actually. She did work for kids' books and magazines and stuff before she got sick. She was crazy good, and we have her artwork up around our house.

I mean, I'm not bad, but . . . the characters Sarah's talking about are Battbutt and Batpig. I made a tiny splash on our school's art scene a couple of years ago when my doodle of Battbutt got me my one and only trip to the principal's office.

I make dumb little comics about their adventures sometimes, but since the principal thing, I've focused more on Batpig. There's less risk.

I actually have a sketchbook where I do most of my Batpig comics. Or just drawings of random stuff. And some more-involved sketching—of *real* things. Life drawing, as my mom called it—but I don't show those to ANYBODY. Not even Abby. Or my dad. It's this awesome beat-up old sketchbook holder that was my mom's. I found it in her things a few years after she died. I don't really remember her dying all that much. Or her, really. But that sketchbook still means a lot to me.

It just feels private, so I keep it that way. For me alone.

Or maybe I'm just worried somebody'll tell me they suck.

NOT FOR PUBLIC
CONSUMPTION

Anyway, I'm kind of shocked my doodles have even landed on Sarah Kennedy's radar. She's always seemed pretty busy with her friends and the whole being-super-popular thing.

Then, while she's looking at me, this *thing* happens to Sarah's face. It morphs and shifts, and suddenly it's all sad-eyed and sincere. I know what's coming. I've seen it a lot lately.

"Anyway . . . how are you *feeling?*" The look of concern on her face makes me want to crawl into a hole and stay there for maybe forever. I'm super uncomfortable with the prolonged we're-all-here-for-you eye contact hold.

I redden. "Oh. Good. Yep. I'm good," I mumble.

"Hang in there, okay?" She nods and gives me a sad smile and turns back around.

I take a deep breath and slide down in my seat. I fold up the talent show flyer and stick it in my back pocket.

I may have dorked out a bit, but my heart didn't seize up.

That's a win in my book.

PROUD BATPIG

5

FINE DINING

"**H**onestly, it was the nicest Jimmy's ever been to me."

This gets a blurt-laugh from Abby. We're eating lunch in our usual spot on the loading dock, where we've kicked a space clear among some fallen leaves. I've never seen the big slide-up door here used for anything, but it backs up to the auditorium stage, so I guess it's for that.

"Oh, Jimmy gets it, y'know? He's such a sensitive young gentleman, with his jar of spit and all." Abby takes a huge bite of her sandwich. She's not what you'd call dainty. She sets it down and tucks her hands inside the sleeves of her hoodie. "How are you not freezing?"

I shrug and chew, the two of us eating in silence for a while. I'm watching two squirrels chase each other across the fence of the football field. They're having a full-on squirrel party.

Isaac used to eat with us out here as well, but he doesn't come around these days. There's no question that Abby's my best friend, but it feels like something big is missing, not getting Isaac's input as well. He's a funny guy.

I mean, it was just this past summer that the three of us made the Great Oreo Pact out at the lake.

Isaac's uncle Anthony had taken us out on Lake Monroe for the day in his speedboat. A perfect late-June day. We started out working on getting Isaac up on skis. Abby and I had figured it out on the last couple of boat trips, but Isaac—skinny little Isaac—had yet to stay up.

I remember him standing on the back of the boat while his uncle got the rope ready, flapping his thin arms around to loosen them up. The life jacket looked huge on him, but then again, so did his swimsuit—it hung well below his knees.

"THIS IS MY DAY, PEOPLE!" He yelled it loud enough that other boats could hear. "Gonna do this. Gonna show you all how it's done." He sniffed. "Might even slalom today." He pointed at Abby and winked.

Four minutes later, he fell trying to get up and forgot to let go of the tow rope. He held on for maybe four hundred feet while he got dragged just under the water—until his senses kicked in and he realized he could just let go.

Climbing back in the boat a few minutes later, he was laughing. His eyes were wide, and his voice sounded weird from all the water he'd taken on. He kind of looked like a wet rat.

"I think I just got a nasal enema."

Later, in a cove called Allen's Creek, where boats anchor and hang out, the three of us were sitting on the back of the boat, our feet in the water. Isaac's uncle was in the front, talking to a friend on the phone. Oreos, chips, and sodas were out as we sat and discussed some of the other boaters. Five or six boats had tied together near us, and it looked like the party was in full swing. Music was drifting over when the wind was right.

"This is awesome. I love this." Isaac is generally a pretty happy guy. "Right? I mean, what's better?"

Abby took a slow drink. "Dummy has a point." I can't remember how it started, but she's been calling Isaac Dummy for a couple of years. Isaac seems to like it.

I was watching the people on the party boat. A few of

them were singing along with the radio. "Is that gonna be us in ten or fifteen years? Are we still gonna be hanging out? Here? Rope swinging?"

Isaac crammed two Oreos in his mouth at once and talked through them. "We'd better be! Three musketeers and all that. Y'know?"

Abby and I nodded, but it wasn't enough for Isaac. "Let's shake on it. Like, in a movie where people cut their palms and swear a blood oath."

I looked at him like he was nuts. "I'm not cutting myself. Sorry."

Isaac waved it away. "Yeah. No. We could do a spit pact. We all spit in our hands and—"

"Gross. No." Abby was having none of that.

Isaac started looking around—he wasn't letting this idea go. Then he grabbed an Oreo. "An Oreo Pact." He untwisted the cookie and used his front teeth to scrape off the little white cream patty. Put it in his damp palm.

I looked at him for a second, then nodded. "That works." We shook, and did our best to smash the white filling in between.

Isaac looked disappointed. "Not gooey enough." He poured some of his Cherry 7UP between our clasped hands, mixing it with the white stuff. "That seems more pacty."

Then he turned and did the same thing with Abby. Then Abby and I did the same.

Isaac hopped to his feet and spoke in a booming voice. "AND WITH THIS ACTION, OUR OREO FRIEND PACT IS OFFICIAL!" Then he took a mouthful of 7UP and sprayed it in the air, so it misted down over the three of us and all over the back of the boat.

"ISAAC!" It was Anthony, and he wasn't happy. Isaac gave us a comical uh-oh look and dove sideways into the dark water.

Back on the loading dock in the cold, Abby takes a long sip of her Dr Pepper and lets out a huge burp.

"Well . . . Ross. At least after today we have definitive proof that Lady Sarah knows you exist. That has to feel good."

"Yeah." I wad up my chip bag and shoot it at the dumpster ten feet away. It misses. "We're a romance for the ages."

"Don't be so hard on yourself. You're just going through a suuuuuper awkward phase right now. It's almost tragic, really—the awkwardness—but you'll grow out of it. Imagine the handsome butterfly that's going to emerge from this horrific cocoon."

I stand up and brush crumbs off of my jeans. "Right?"

I hop off the dock. "But, ugh, you should've seen the pity on Sarah's face. It was . . . I really don't enjoy being 'the Sick Kid.' To her or to anybody, you know?" I walk over and put the chip bag in the dumpster. "I wish Linda would've kept her mouth shut."

Months ago, when we got the diagnosis, my stepmom texted one of her girlfriends. Who texted about thirty of *her* girlfriends—and then Linda's phone was blowing up and everyone in town knew. Including everyone at school. Including Sarah Kennedy.

I'm still not sure what Linda was thinking. She might as well have pulled out a bullhorn and announced it to the world.

Abby's always telling me to stop worrying about being the Sick Kid. Or in her words, "I don't know why you let that stuff chew you up so much."

I lean on the dock thinking about ways to disable my stepmother's iPhone.

A big gust of wind throws our hair around. Abby's especially. The cold and wind make my eye sting.

Then I remember the flyer in my pocket. "Did you hear about the talent show? Sarah gave me a flyer about it."

"Yeah, I saw one in the bathroom."

I twist around and look at her. "You should do it! Play that one solo I like!" I mime playing the viola.

"Maybe. If Sarah runs the show on the up-and-up." She sniffs and wipes her nose on her sleeve. I can tell she's not 100 percent on the Sarah train. "But maybe you're onto something . . . Kids these days can't get enough of viola solos, am I right?"

I laugh. "Whatever. You're super good. You could come up with something cool." I've sat and drawn for count-less hours while she practices.

"Hmmm. Let me think about it." She puts a red curl in her mouth to chew. She chews her hair when she's deep in thought. "You should do something. For the show. It'd be an easy in with Princess Sarah."

"Okay. Like what? Drawing isn't much of a spectacle."

"Yeah . . ." She puts another curl in her mouth for extra thinking power. "It's really too bad you suck at everything."

I ignore her, and we sit there for a while watching the squirrels.

I sniff loudly. My nose is freezing. "Have you talked to Isaac at all?"

She lets out a puff of air. "Nope. I mean, I see him in the halls, but we don't really talk." She sniffs, louder. "We've been officially ghosted."

"It's weird."

Abby nods her head and looks away.

Isaac's a video game fanatic, so when we'd hang out as a threesome, it was usually at his house—in his awesome basement. He and his brothers have every game and gaming system known to man. And, while Abby isn't huge into video games, she liked the Nalibotskys' pinball machine. And their popcorn machine. And Isaac.

I always kind of had this feeling that Abby and Isaac might date when we were older. I started calling them Ron and Hermione for a while until Abby gave me a nipple twist so hard she almost pulled it off.

Then . . . I got sick. And he slowly stopped coming around. Or inviting us over. Or texting. Or responding to texts. It makes me sick to my stomach if I think about it too much.

The timing with me getting sick and him vanishing seems too exact to be a coincidence. That has to be it, but it's really . . . I don't know. It sucks.

Abby blows hot air between her hands. "He's hanging out a lot with Chris Stemmle. Eats lunch with him and that whole *Fortnite* crew."

"Yeah. I've seen."

Chris Stemmle is a guy I'd always thought was *at least* unfriendly and possibly a real jerk. I don't get it.

"Meh." This is Abby's couldn't-care-less sound, but I'm not buying it. I think she feels hurt too. "His loss."

I brush some Doritos dust off my jacket. "I guess."

Just then, a huge gust of wind kicks up a bunch of leaves. Abby covers her head with one arm and starts shoving things into her bag.

"Nope! No! Screw this! Winter is coming, and I'm going inside!"

I grab my pack and follow her. We duck in the side door by the auditorium, where a bunch of the band members are eating in the hall. Abby knows them all—she's first chair viola, after all. I'm still not entirely sure what that means, but I know it means a lot to her. She always looks the happiest when she's practicing.

Abby takes a moment to pick a leaf out of her hair and check her reflection in the announcements box. She seems happy with the crazy, windblown mess she sees there. "Perfection!" she says, throwing her shoulders back and strutting through her fellow band kids like she's a model on a runway.

It gets a laugh.

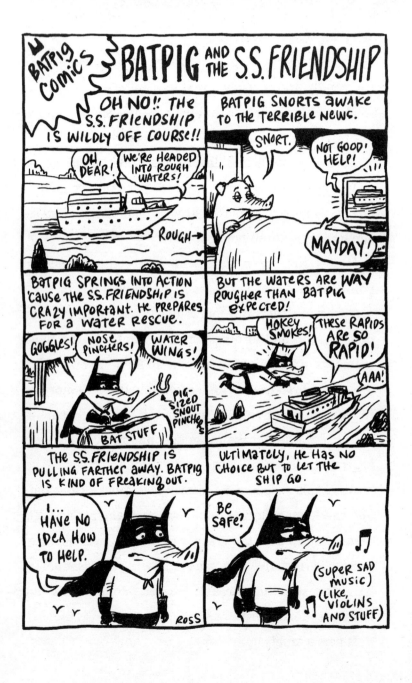

6

BACK TO THE BAD

Bad Day #2 was Diagnosis Day, when I learned whether the thing in my head was benign (what we were hoping for) or malignant (what we were most definitely *not* hoping for).

A couple of weeks earlier, we'd gone into the hospital super early one morning for a biopsy, where the doctors took a little chunk of my tumor: They knocked me out and shoved a big needle through my eyelid to get a sample . . . and then I lay in bed and watched Netflix all day. Isaac and Abby came over that day, but even then, Isaac seemed like he wasn't looking at me or my bandaged face when we talked.

I had to wear a big patch for a couple of days and got a black eye afterward, but if I'm being totally honest, the black eye was kind of cool. I kind of liked the looks I got with it, like I'd been in a fight. Like I was some kind of brawler.

But this day—Diagnosis Day—was different, so it gets the Bad Day title. It was still summer, and that morning was so hot and humid, it felt like my clothes were soggy. It was a Tuesday, so my dad had to pull some major strings, but he got the morning off from trial prep to take me.

My dad, Linda, and I piled into Linda's Grand Cherokee and had a quiet morning drive to Dr. Sheffler's office. The kind of drive where Linda—in the passenger seat, unsure of what to talk about—chose to read random billboards and store signs out loud.

"Plassman Plumbing—We Get Things Moving."

"ONE DAY ONLY—Half-Price Mattresses."

"Gyros as big as your face!"

I'm not sure why she thought this was better than silence—my grandmother, Gammy, does the same thing sometimes—but Linda kept going until I wanted to bang my head against the window.

When we arrived at Dr. Sheffler's office, he looked flustered. His hair was messed up in a few places, where there was usually never a hair out of place.

"Okay." He looked us each in the eye. "I'm not going

to sugarcoat this. We got the results back, and this is an aggressive tumor. A mucoepidermoid carcinoma of the lacrimal gland. It's an incredibly rare tumor, as well."

We all just stared.

"I honestly didn't think I'd ever see one in my career."

At that point, my head ever so gently dislodged from my neck and began to float toward the ceiling. At least that's how it felt.

As my dad and Linda started asking about things like prognosis and outlook and treatment, my balloon head kept slowly rising toward the fluorescent light above me. It was the weirdest feeling—like I was watching from above while someone else heard all about how dangerous this tumor was. And about how one of the other doctors in his office had dealt with one of these before. And how she'd agreed to meet with us.

He went to get her, and we waited in stunned silence until they both came back.

Dr. Inzer was a severe-looking woman. She was super thin and had incredibly straight, long black hair. With her lab coat on, she reminded me of a black-and-white Popsicle.

She was about as warm as one too, but I was willing to forgive her personality if she could help me.

"Hello, Ross. Mr. and Mrs. Maloy." She sat on a stool next to Dr. Sheffler with posture that would have made a drill sergeant look lazy. "I've looked through Ross's file, and I'm here to tell you I can help."

My dad let out a breath like he'd been holding it for weeks. "Oh, thank God."

Inzer gave him what I *think* was supposed to be a smile.

"Now, you may not like what I have to say, but you need to know that this is an extremely aggressive tumor." She looked me in the eye, and I swear I shivered.

"Here's what we need to do." She glanced at Dr. Sheffler, then scooted her stool toward me. She lifted her hand—an insanely long-fingered hand—up to my eye.

"We'll remove the entire eye and socket." She twisted her clawlike fingers around my whole eye area to demonstrate—like an ice cream scoop.

"That's really the only way to get safe margins."

She gave me another alien smile. Maybe it was supposed to be comforting? "We'll fit you for a prosthetic for that part of your face, of course. And then we'll follow up with radiation."

She sat back, ready for questions.

We all sat there blinking for a moment. Even Dr. Sheffler looked stunned. I can't speak for anyone else, but my blood had turned to ice. It was the bluntest delivery of horrible news I can imagine. Like she was telling me she was going to pop a zit on my forehead.

My dad sat back, and I couldn't tell if he was going to yell at her or pass out. "When . . . when would you . . . do this?"

Dr. Inzer didn't blink. "I have an opening Thursday morning. "

My dad's face fell. He looked to Dr. Sheffler for help, then back. "In two days?"

Inzer reached down and straightened the edge of her lab coat. Gently settled her hands together in her lap. "I'm terribly sorry. I know this is a shock, but time is absolutely of the essence."

I wasn't sure I could speak. "Is that the only . . . the only way?"

Dr. Sheffler sat up and started to try to soften the blow. "Well, I'm sure we can look into—"

Dr. Inzer put a hand on his arm, and a look passed

between them. She looked annoyed. "In my opinion, Ross, it is our only option. I've dealt with this before. This is a serious tumor and needs to be handled as such. To be frank, your life is more important than your vision."

Linda swallowed, loudly. "So, his vision? It would . . ."

Dr. Inzer scooted back a bit. "Obviously, there would be no vision in the resected eye." She sighed—the first sign that there was a human in there. "The unfortunate thing is that radiation will almost certainly cause vision loss in the left eye, as well."

"Jesus!" My dad stood up, then immediately sat back down. "How much vision loss?"

"Total. Unfortunately." In her defense, Dr. Inzer looked like it genuinely pained her to say it. Dr. Sheffler just looked uncomfortable.

We all sat in silence for a bit. Linda fished a wadded-up Kleenex out of her purse and dabbed at her nose. For some reason I couldn't feel the chair under my butt. It was that floating feeling again.

Apparently when bad things happen, you feel like you're floating.

Finally, the doctor spoke again. "I am so sorry. But you need to know how serious the situation is. I wish I could give you better news."

I was wishing the same thing. Or that this was some really twisted joke. Like she was going to tell me I was on a prank show.

But she didn't. I wasn't.

Yet again, leaving that office is a blur to me. I saw Dr. Inzer write down the name of a few books we should look up online. She handed the piece of paper to Linda while my dad was talking quietly with Dr. Sheffler. Linda only half tucked it in her coat pocket, so I grabbed it when she wasn't looking.

The first book was something about "accepting a new normal." The second title had the words "living with disfigurement" in it.

Wow.

I quietly tucked the paper back into Linda's coat and walked outside to wait for them.

Later, my dad took me over to Abby's. She'd been texting, and I hadn't responded. Telling her by text would have felt wrong.

She met me at the front door. "So?"

I gave her the best smile I could. "Let's go for a walk. Down to the creek or something."

Her face fell, and I'm pretty sure her summer tan faded a bit.

■ ■ ■

There are some fields behind Abby's subdivision that lead down to a small creek, where we've spent hours splashing around and catching crawdads. It's kind of our spot. Or one of them, anyway.

We climbed over the rail fence and set off into the waist-high weeds and grass at the back of their property. I walked quietly for a minute before I started in.

"The news isn't, um . . . good."

Abby watched me while I grabbed a big stick out of the path and threw it to the side. "So, it's cancer?"

"Yeah." I let out a slow breath. "It is. And it's some rare kind or something. Of course."

"What kind is it?"

"I don't know." We both hopped down a small embankment. "I don't really want to know. At least not right this second. It's a mugga-mugga epi-carny lacri-cancer or something. It's super bad and aggressive, apparently. Whatever that means."

I heard Abby behind me and realized she'd stopped.

"Oh, Ross." I turned around, and she had watery eyes. "I'm sorry." She put her arms around me in a big hug. I felt tears stinging my eyes and nose.

I told her what I remembered about the specialist and all the horrifying eye stuff as we took off our socks and shoes and waded into the creek. Everything looked . . . different. I was looking at the world through post-cancer-diagnosis eyes.

I wondered if this was the last time I'd be able to look around these woods.

When I was finished, Abby sat on her rock and wrapped her arms around her knees. "Have you told Isaac yet?"

I shook my head. "No. I'll call him."

She closed her eyes for a few seconds. "So, are you . . ." Then she kind of ran out of gas, like she didn't know what she wanted to say.

I looked up at the trees above us.

"Right?"

We sat that way, quietly, for a while.

I think Bad Day #2 was the longest I've ever heard Abby go without talking.

7

LASER BEAMS
AND FRENCH FRIES

Back in the present, my dad's waiting behind the wheel when I come out of school. Time for my second treatment. It's only a few minutes to the proton radiation center, but he's been through McDonald's to pick up Cokes and a couple orders of fries. "For sustenance," he says, cramming a handful in his mouth.

I straddle one of my dad's big accordion files crammed full of legal papers in the footwell.

He shifts the car into gear. "You ready for Day Two?"

I pick out a single fry. "Do I have a choice?"

"No. No, I guess you don't." He washes the wad of fries down with a sip of Coke. "You okay?"

I think about that for a minute, watching some guy rake bright orange leaves out of his yard.

"I think so. I mean, I guess so?" I look over at him, and he still looks tired. "Are *you* okay?"

He looks over, surprised. "Me? Yeah. Just busy. Why?"

I give a quick shrug. "I dunno." A big gust of wind comes along and sends half of the guy's neatly raked pile of leaves flying. "You've been through it before. I mean, I'm sure it was awful—with Mom. It had to be. And now it's happening again. I feel . . . guilty."

My dad is facing forward, but I see a look flash across his face that's almost angry. "Ross . . . no. I don't ever want you to feel that way. Don't even think that. You didn't ask for this."

I lean my head back. "I know. It just doesn't seem fair."

He turns a corner a little wide, distracted. "Oh, it's not." He gives me a funny smile. "But who ever said life is fair?"

I take a long drink.

"Nobody, I guess."

"Ya got that right." He drives for a few moments in

silence. "You and I are in it now. Together. Our job is just to roll with the punches."

I grab another fry. "Punch rolling. Got it."

"Life punches, we roll." He raises his eyebrows. "Right, dude?"

He leans over toward me. He's being dorky to be funny.

"I told you not to say dude."

"Okay, *dude*." He leans in more. Raises his eyebrows farther. He's such a dad.

I give him half a smile just to stop him, and something pops into my head.

"Hey . . . Would it be totally weird if I wanted to go in and do this by myself? Like, I don't know . . . so I'm not like a little kid?"

He sits back, surprised, but thinks for a second. "No, that's not weird." He nods. "I get that."

"You sure? I'm not even sure why I'm asking."

He looks out of his window for a bit. We're in the parking lot outside the radiation center. When he looks back, I see his eyes are shinier than usual. Teary. I wasn't really going for a touching moment here, but it looks like it's heading that way.

"Have I told you how proud I am of you?"

Oh boy. "Yes, you have, Dad. About a thousand times."

"Ha." His laugh is wet. "Right. But I am. The way

you're handling this, it's . . . Your mom would be—" His throat catches, and he shakes his head. Then he's wiping his eyes and waving me out of the car. "Okay. Whatever. Out! Out! Before I start blubbering and snotting all over the place."

I open the door and climb out. "Too late!"

In the lobby, Jerry is in the same chair with a cup of coffee like he never left. He looks up from his AARP magazine. "There he is. Young Ross." His voice is so gravelly it sounds like it hurts. "How're you doing today?"

I sit on a couch across from him. I waggle my hand. So-so.

"I hear ya. You come straight from school?"

I nod. He nods back.

I busy myself digging around through my school folders.

"So. What kind?" Jerry asks. He's rolling his magazine up in his big hands.

I look up. "What? What kind of school?"

"Your cancer. Where is it? Mine's here." He points a large, crooked finger at his lap. This stops me cold, and he waves a big hand at me. "Never mind. I was just bein' nosy. Nosy old man." He chuckles, and it turns into a loud, wheezy coughing fit.

I wait until I'm pretty sure he isn't going to die. "My eye."

Jerry wipes his mouth and chin with a yellowed handkerchief. He sniffs a couple of times. "I wondered. Is that where you got this?" He points at the middle of his forehead.

Between my eyebrows, I have a scar. It looks like an inch-long slit right about where your brow would crease if you were mad.

I nod. "Yeah. That's where they shot BBs into my skull. So the machine knows where to put the beam."

There are actually four scars, but the rest are hidden in my hair. For the moment, at least.

Jerry's nodding. "It's like your own personal dime slot." He rubs his forehead.

"Dime slot?"

He waves his big hand. "Like a coin slot. Where you'd put a dime in a pay phone." He raises his furry eyebrows and chuckles. "Pay phone. Okay. Never mind. Your age, it's probably more of a 'Harry Potter scar,' I'd guess."

This surprises me. "You know about Harry Potter?"

He laughs and unrolls his magazine. "I'm old, son, not dead! And I have grandkids. I've seen a couple of the movies." He gives me another look-over. "Is that why that one eye is shut too?"

"Yeah." I look away.

The hallway doors fly open, and Frank walks in. He stops for a second to survey the situation.

"Okay, Ross. Let's us young people go have some fun with protons. Leave the old man to read his old-people magazines."

I grab my bag and follow him, giving Jerry a wave.

He lifts a hand and smiles. "See ya round, Dime Slot!"

Frank looks over at me. "Dime Slot?"

I roll my eyes and point at my scar. Frank barks a laugh.

"Love it."

"U2?!?"

Frank looks disappointed. He sighs, staring at the CD in his hands.

"Okay, Ross. I was . . . This is Dad Rock, but it's . . . it's better than last time. Sort of . . ." His voice dies off as he slowly turns and plods toward the radio shelf. Like he's dragging his feet through quicksand.

I spent some time digging through my dad's CD collection last night, and I was pretty sure I'd picked a winner.

Callie hasn't put the U-lock piece down yet, so I can still kind of talk. "Just so I don't let you down in the future, what exactly were you hoping I'd bring?"

This stops Frank. He comes back to the metal table. "U2's fine. They are. They're a good, solid band. But don't you ever go off-roading? Musically, I mean? Listen to some stuff that's off the beaten path? Or on the edges of the path, at least."

I just lie there, as I can't move. "I guess not."

"Okay. Tomorrow I want you to bring something you love, but you're not sure anyone else would like. Something off-the-wall. Something maybe a little dangerous."

I wait a second before I respond. "Well, I would . . . but CDs are kinda for . . . old people."

Frank stares at me.

"Did you hear what he said, Callie? Did you hear that? I told you there were signs of life in this one." As Callie reaches over with the mouthpiece, he steps aside. "Callie kept saying you were a big dud, but I said no. I said, 'You watch. This kid has an inner something—we just have to keep digging.'"

Callie smiles and shakes her head at me. "If you'd like him removed, blink twice."

Frank turns and walks to the CD player, waving his hands theatrically. "Here you go, Ross! Here comes your stadium-ready, corporate-approved Jock Rock! Off we go to where the streets have no name!"

Callie checks the placement of my blob of blue nose clay and tells me not to mind him.

The treatment feels long today, and I'm not sure why. There are several times when I realize my eye is drifting and I curse myself out in my head. Last thing I need is a deep-fried eyeball.

FRIED EYEBALL
(WITH A SIDE OF
MARINARA

As we're walking out, I tell Frank he should bring some of his CDs in tomorrow, as I've always had an interest in antiques.

"Says the kid who brought in an album from thirty years ago." Frank punches the button on the electric doors, and we walk into the mostly empty waiting room. Jerry must be getting zapped in the other treatment room.

"You watch. I'll have you off that spoon-fed Top Forty junk in no time."

Just then, the receptionist calls to me and tells me Dr. Throckton—the Man with All the Answers—wants to see me if I have a minute. Two minutes later, I'm sitting across from him in an exam room, and I learn things are about to go from bad to catastrophic.

8

HATS
AND HOW TO HATE THEM

'm at Abby's. There are three wide-brimmed hats spread out on her bed.

"Boy." She has her hands on her hips and blows a curl out of her face. "Wow . . . This is some choice."

I groan.

"Tell me again what exactly the doctor said?"

So, I tell her for the third time how Dr. Throckton had pulled me into his office after my treatment to announce:

I have to start wearing a hat. A big wide-brimmed one, to keep the sun off my face. Apparently—because of all the radiation I'm getting from the treatments—I need extra protection from UV rays.

And not just when I'm outside. Oh, no.

Everywhere.

Indoors. Everywhere there are windows. At home. In the car. At the hospital.

IN SCHOOL.

"Doctor's orders," he'd said. "The risks from sun exposure are blahfully blahblah. Not to blahm, but blah a blahgerous blahtuation . . ." The rest of our talk is a blur to me, because all I heard in my head was panic. Rushing blood. Brain static. All chances at being a halfway normal seventh grader are slipping away from me.

Now Abby and I are studying the only wide-brimmed hats my dad and I could find at the mall. My dad insisted on getting all three, so I could think about it.

"What am I gonna do? Throckton's, like, the smartest guy in the world, so if he says I need it . . . but . . ." My shoulders slump.

"Ooh! Look at this one," Abby says, grabbing a hat. She's wearing these green, furry monster gloves that she found at the Halloween store—her new favorite find. "It has a little . . . a little cape in the back here." She pulls a strap, and a flap unfolds. "To keep the tsetse flies off your neck. That's smart." She places it delicately on my head. Tightens the chinstrap.

"Okay . . ." She steps back and looks me up and down. "You look like you should be wrestling crocodiles on Animal Planet, but that's not *all* bad."

"Fantastic." I take off the hat and put on the one that makes me think of *Gilligan's Island*.

She smiles. "Heyyyyy. There's my Little Buddy!"

We've binged all the adventures of the S.S. *Minnow* at least twice over the years. In her basement, over Cheetos and Dr Pepper.

I try the third hat on. It's a straw cowboy-hat-looking thing with the edges of the brim rolled up.

"Okay, that one really isn't that bad. I mean . . . it's *horrible*, but it's less horrible than the others. Pardner."

I walk over to the floor-length mirror on her closet door . . . and see a cowboy staring back.

I just need a piece of straw sticking out of my mouth. "I look like I'm going to a hoedown."

Abby pushes the other hats aside and sits on the edge of her bed. "It's not that bad. You'll get through it. Maybe you should draw one of your characters on it or write *DOCTOR'S ORDERS* in really big print."

I fall into her papasan chair. "I might. Or *Prescription-Strength Hat.*"

We sit in silence for a minute.

"On the plus side," she says, "it'll cover things up when you start losing your hair."

I sigh and look around the room. It looks like Halloween in here, but it has nothing to do with it being two days before Halloween. Her room looks like this year-round. Every inch of wall space is covered in eBay purchases— posters and photos—representing her two biggest passions. Monster/horror movies and some weird band called Vampire Weekend. Godzilla, King Kong, Franken- stein's monster, and a giant tarantula are all looking down at us from the walls.

Back to the hair loss, Abby's tried several times to talk me into shaving my head—ahead of it falling out—saying it would be "EPIC." I've assured her that I'm not going for "epic" the way she is. She even offered to shave hers along with me. She seems to have a hard time understanding my whole wanting-to-blend-in thing.

Her mom leans into the room. "How's it going in here?" She sees me and gets that sad, sincere look on her face. Concern Face.

"You doing okay, Ross? With the treatments?"

I nod and give her a big smile. "Yep. Getting along. Yep." A brief pause. "Yeppers."

I really need to figure out how to respond to these questions.

She nods back. "Okay. Good. No Isaac?"

Abby shakes her head, and her mom makes a thinking face. Makes a *hmmmm* sound. Then her comfortable mom smile is back. "Want me to throw in a Totino's for you guys?"

Abby lights up. "Ooh! Do we have triple cheese?"

"I'll check. I think so." She knocks the wood of the door frame twice, ducking out.

Abby catches me glaring at my reflection in her mirror. I'm not liking what I see there.

Cowboy Ross. He of the Goofy Hat.

"It's gonna be fine, Ross."

I nod. Sort of a half nod.

"I'm telling you, Ross," Abby says, "you need to grab this thing by the reins. If you have to be the weird guy, own it."

I put my head back and let out a long groan.

SURLY BATPIG

9

GIDDYUP

The next day, I'm not prepared to deal with the bus in a cowboy hat, so Linda gives me a ride to school. She tries to make me feel better during the drive. Granted, it's in her Linda Way.

"Maybe this could be a whole new look for you, you know?" She waves her venti green tea at my hat. (Of course we stopped at Starbucks. Bucky's. Whatever.) "Own it. Be Ross the Hat Guy inside and out. Tip the brim at girls like a movie rancher." She mimes it. "Like that."

I know Linda is only trying to help, and she's saying the same stuff Abby did, but I feel sick.

It's raining, but I ask Linda to drop me off before we get to the parking lot. I cut across the soggy lawn. What's a couple of wet feet compared to impending social death?

Abby's waiting at the bike rack by the front door,

wiping off her viola case. She studies me and refuses to feel sorry for me. "It's just a hat, Ross. Seriously. You look like your dog died."

I get a few funny looks and a handful of pointed fingers as I walk down the hall to my locker. One kid gives me a thumbs-up and a loud "NOICE!" I hear "Get along, little doggy!" as I pass the biology room. But the biggest reaction comes in Ms. Bayer's class. I've been dreading this one.

"What the . . ."

Jimmy.

"Not cool!" he sputters. "How come you get to wear a hat, Butt Crack?"

"It's not by choice." I point at the front where I really did end up writing *DOCTOR'S ORDERS* like Abby suggested. My dad wasn't happy about the ruined hat but decided to let it slide.

Jimmy scrunches his face up. "Whatever. I wore one last year, and Mr. Phillips took it. I had hat hair for two days!"

I choose not to mention that he has a pretty serious case of hat hair right now.

My eye is killing me, so I grab one of my little eye drop vials and (as quick as I can) put in a couple of drops, wiping away the gooey liquid before it can dry there and get all crusty. I've had a few days where I get home and it looks like I rubbed a glazed donut on my eye.

I realize Jimmy's still watching me. "What's up with you and those stupid drops?"

I tuck the vial back in my jeans.

"I don't have tears in that eye. They took out the gland that makes tears during my surgery, so I have to use 'em."

He stares, chomping away. He looks around and quickly pulls his spit jar out of his desk. Lets fly and then tucks it away.

"Yeah? Or, what?"

"If I go very long, it starts to sting really bad. Burns. So . . . drops. And it stings super bad when it's open."

Jimmy stares at me long enough I wonder if he's stalled out. "That why you hold it closed?"

I nod.

He swallows. "That sucks."

"Yeah." I shrug. "It kind of does."

Then he turns away, and I hear him mutter something under his breath. Was it . . . *Cowboy*?

Great. I mean, I guess it's a better nickname than Butt Crack. I guess.

I glance back over, but he just sits there staring forward with a big, stupid, mean look on his face.

During fourth period, I feel a sudden, pounding need to go to the bathroom. Mr. Beaulieu gives me a hall pass, and I make it with only minutes to spare.

On my way back to class, I'm about to turn down another empty hallway when Isaac comes around the corner, right in front of me. I think we're both caught off guard, because we stop.

"Hey . . . Isaac." Why am I suddenly nervous? He's one of my two best friends in the world.

He looks a little trapped. There are no other students to dash off to or hide behind. "Heyyy, Ross."

I'm not sure what to say, so I say, "Bathroom?"

He laughs, but it seems like an uncomfortable laugh. "Yep."

"Me too." I pat the hall pass against my palm. "Hey. How are you doing on *Annihilation: Moon*?"

Isaac puts one of his sticklike arms up and rubs the back of his neck. "Oh. Good. I'm . . . almost done. Have you done the whole crater challenge?"

This is literally our first conversation in forever, and I feel myself light up. "Yeah! I just finished the crater! We should get together and play sometime! Maybe—"

He cuts me off by holding clenched fists together in front of him and doing a little dance/shuffle. "Ross, buddy, I'm about to pee myself. But we'll get together soon! I swear."

I nod. "Yeah. Yeah, okay." And he's past me. I don't think he meant that about getting together soon. I know what a brush-off feels like.

I turn around in time to see him duck into the boys' room, and suddenly there's a big pit in my stomach. Like somebody took a melon baller and scooped it out.

I'm slowly walking past the AV room when John Meeker sees me and leans out. He points at my head and sings in a snarly voice, "Hey, hey! Save a horse, ride a cowboy!"

I think it's from a country song. I just give him a smile and a thumbs-up and get back to class.

By the end of the day, most everybody's seen the hat and gotten their "Yeehaw!" "Saddle up!" and "Halloween's tomorrow!" comments out.

Nobody knocks it off my head or laughs in my face the way I'd dreaded. In fact, most kids just kind of look for a moment and then . . . accept it. Cancer Kids get hats, and that's that, I guess.

When my dad picks me up to take me to my treatment, my spirits are kind of up, unbelievably. For a brief moment, I feel like there's hope in the world.

■　■　■

Frank stops in his tracks when he sees me in the waiting room, his face suddenly looks dead serious like something's wrong.

"Ah'm afraid this town ain't big enough fer the two of us, Sheriff."

I groan. "Hilarious. Did you bring this amazing music you keep going on about?" I duck past him and hit the button for the automatic doors.

He catches up. "You joke, but your real education begins today, my young Padawan. Prepare to have your mind expanded and potentially blown."

Once I'm on the table and the mask is in place, Frank holds a CD up in front of me. It has scrawly writing on it.

"Made it last night. Think you can handle it?"

Callie steps in with my mouthpiece. "Oh, no. This doesn't have your band on it, does it?"

Frank's eyelids go to half-mast. "Only the first couple of songs are Ripe Sponge. Then it's just a hodgepodge. A mishmash, if you will."

"Ripe Sponge?" I have time to ask, before the mouthpiece goes in. "What's that?"

"Ripe Sponge! That's my band!"

He goes over and rattles the CD into the tray, hits Play, and ducks around the corner.

Callie looks at me while she fits the mouthpiece onto the table. "If I'm being honest, his band isn't terrible. But I'd never tell him that." Then she reminds me not to look away from the X, pats my arm, and walks out of the room.

Frank doesn't hold back on the volume today.

First there's a heavy drum. A fast, low thumping that goes on longer than it seems like it should. But then come some other drums. Louder and a little messy.

Next is a bass line, lower than the drums. I feel the music in my chest, and it goes on like this for a bit. I can't tap my feet—I have to stay as still as possible—but I'm tapping them in my head. It's the kind of beat that makes you want to move around.

Finally, a guitar comes in, ripping a hole in the middle of the song. It's cool and spooky and smoky and thrilling all at the same time.

I'm hooked.

The singer comes in—is it Frank? I can't understand all the words, but who cares?—and it gets even better. I think the song is about a girl and maybe flying . . . and there's something about evil nachos, unless I'm hearing it wrong.

But the lyrics don't even matter that much.

I just love this song. Instantly. Completely.

I'm really not sure why the music is hitting me like this on this particular day—like it's sinking into me rather than bouncing off—but it is.

I mean, I've heard music before. Good music. Why today?

Maybe my defenses are down because of "radiation nerves"? Maybe it's just a new kind of music I'm not used to—like it's *my* kind of music and it's been waiting for me out there. Maybe the proton beam is accidentally zapping my brain, and I'm having some kind of seconds-to-death moment of clarity.

Or maybe I just need it now.

I'm not sure, but it's lighting me up in a way I haven't experienced before.

The next few songs are heavier than anything I've heard on KZAQ and three times harder than anything in my dad's collection, but I love them, and I want more.

I can't keep the smile off my face, mouthpiece and all. As I walk out afterward, I realize I haven't thought about my stupid hat for at least fifteen minutes.

10

BAD HALLOWEEN

The second day with the hat—Halloween—goes less well.

This is what we call an understatement.

I meet Abby by the bike rack—she's wearing her black jack-o'-lantern shirt and a headband with demon horns—and before we even reach our lockers, I can tell something is off in the halls. Nobody makes a hat comment, but several people turn around with uh-oh-here-he-comes faces. Ricky Stevenson, an eighth grader with crazy-tall hair, lets out a startled laugh when he sees me—then stifles it behind his hand and ducks into the art room like he committed a crime.

While I'm grabbing a folder from my locker, I catch one girl—Bethany something?—whispering in her friend's ear. She has her hand covering her mouth, and they're both looking at me, the international signal for We're Talking About You.

I shut my locker and turn to Abby. She's messing with the pull strings of her Vampire Weekend tour hoodie.

"What's up?"

She looks back at me. "Chicken butt."

"Hilarious. Why is everyone looking at me?"

She pushes off the wall and heads down the crowded hall. "I'm sure it's the hat, ding-dong."

I follow her, watching other students as we go. She squeezes between a couple of big football players to her locker. Starts working the combination. She swings the door open between us.

I'm not buying it. My Spidey senses are tingling. I see another person stepping sideways to get a look at me from behind someone's backpack.

I lean in to look Abby in the eyes. "You swear you don't know anything?"

"Ross. Stop it. You're a minor celebrity now. Hat Kid. Try to enjoy it." She gives me a goofy smile and pats my shoulder awkwardly. "Don't go mental on me. 'Kay? I gotta go, or I'll be late." She gives me a punch on the arm. "Seriously. You'll be fine." Then she's gone. Swallowed up in the morning chaos.

My palms are starting to sweat. This isn't good.

■ ■ ■

By lunch I'm in a full panic. You'd think I'm walking around naked the way people are looking at me. I've had that nightmare, and this is worse.

I asked a couple of kids in my class about it, but they all played dumb—and not very convincingly. My brain is spinning like a top when I meet Abby at the loading dock. She's unpacking her lunch and looks up.

"Hey, Wink!" Normally I don't mind the eye-related jokes, but today I'm in no mood.

I throw my lunch down. "What is going on? People are looking at me like I have six heads."

She sets her sandwich down.

"Ross! I swear I have no idea! I doubt it's anything, but I'll ask around if it'll make you feel better."

I sit down on the top step and tip my head back. Groan.

"Take some deep breaths. You're spinning out, buddy."

After a couple of minutes, I look back down and stare at my crumpled lunch bag.

"If it makes you feel better, I heard Sean Meekins barfed in gym class."

"Seriously?"

She nods. "Yep. Halfway up the big rope. It splattered and got a bunch of people. Including Hannigan."

I can't help picturing Coach Hannigan scrambling

not to get yarf on his precious sneakers. He loves those sneakers.

"Okay. That . . . is kind of awesome, I guess."

She asks me about the new Language Arts assignment, and then we talk about some new Vampire Weekend shirt she found on eBay, and about whether we're too old for trick-or-treating.

By the time lunch is over and we're throwing out our trash—Abby has me smiling again.

11

NOT RIGHT

More weird stares follow me the rest of the day, which makes me bonkers. Why the acceptance one day and now all the staring? It doesn't make any sense.

By the time my dad picks me up for my treatment, I'm actually looking forward to it. Anything is better than the stares.

Frank cues up the mix from where I left it the day before. He and Callie strap me down, and I'm off.

Despite the risk of zapping my eyeball—or the knowledge that I'm getting nuked like a microwave corn dog— I'm able to relax and get into the songs.

The second song—a fast one with some guy screaming about needing "the cure for what ails me"—fits my
mood perfectly.

The next one is kind of slow and sappy, which surprises me coming from Frank, but even that one takes
me on a ride. Gets me out of my funk and brain frenzy
for a bit.

Before I leave, Frank hands me the mixtape. "For
extracurricular listening. If you want."

My dad brings my Deadpool costume in a plastic bag,
and we head to Abby's house.

It feels weird, walking up to Abby's place. For the last
few years, we've always started our night at Isaac's and
ended at Abby's. Things change, I guess.

Abby meets me at the front door, and I can tell something isn't right. She looks strung out. Even weirder, she
isn't in a costume.

As we pass the kitchen, her parents are huddled over
the counter having what looks like a "serious conversation." Her mom gives me a quick wave, then turns back
to Mr. Peterson.

I feel butterflies coming to life in my stomach.

In Abby's room, she tells me to sit down. She's chewing her hair, which might not be a good sign. I drop my

backpack and the bag with my costume and sit down carefully at her desk. I'm moving slowly.

Abby comes over and sits on the corner of her bed near my chair. Runs a hand through her hair.

"Okay. Ross." She looks up at the ceiling. She grimaces. "I think I figured out why everyone was staring."

I notice her phone in her hand. She's holding it so tight her knuckles are white.

"So . . . Stacy Tyler just sent me these . . . things. They're pictures that somebody made. I don't know who made them, and neither does Stacy. She really doesn't. I believe her."

"Okayyyy." My ears are ringing, but I try to remain calm.

She sighs. "I guess these were flying around all day. On Instagram. By text. Nobody sent them to me, 'cause, y'know . . . we're friends and all."

I can't take this. "What are you talking about?"

She tips her head back.

"Apparently these went around to a bunch of people last night and today—to a *lot* of people. They're, like . . . memes."

I swallow. "I've been *memed*?"

She laughs, but not a ha-ha laugh. More of a one-puff, sad laugh. "Yeah. There were three of them. They're . . ."

She's not sure what to say, and that isn't a situation Abby finds herself in often. "They aren't funny, Ross. They're bad."

I'm trying to brace for impact, like a new diagnosis is coming.

I hold out my hand, and she gives me her phone.

The first image in her text feed is my sixth-grade yearbook photo. Somebody has drawn a really rough version of a cowboy hat on my head.

Relief washes over me. It's not that bad. Kind of mean-spirited, but I was expecting way worse.

I scroll to the next image.

Someone has spent some time on this one. Really put in the effort. It's a drawing of my head on a super skinny old guy in a hospital gown—he looks awful—holding on to an IV stand.

But the third is the winner. The icing on the cake. The pièce de résistance, as they say.

It's the simplest of the three. Somebody's taken an existing cartoon and changed the words. Or really, just one word.

It's a black-and-white panel cartoon of Death in an airport. It must have been taken from a magazine—*The New Yorker* maybe. My parents get that magazine, and it looks like that style. In it, Death—his face hidden in a hood and holding his big ax thing—is standing in front of a limo. He's holding a sign, looking for his next customer.

I sit staring at it for a bit, and I can feel my throat and chest tightening. My face is getting hot.

So, Death is waiting for me? Is that what they're implying? That I'm dying? Is that the *joke*?

"Ross, look, it's—" Abby starts.

I interrupt. "Is this . . . How is this at all funny? Is it *supposed* to be funny?"

Abby takes the phone from me. "I don't know. Stacy

doesn't even know who did them. They're just . . . going around. I basically beat her over the head to get her to show 'em to me."

I stand back up, 'cause I'm not sure what else to do. "Who would . . ." I feel heat rolling up through my body, starting from my toes. "Like an enemy, or . . ."

My hands are shaking.

"Ross," Abby says, "we'll figure out who did these. And my parents said we should go to the principal, first thing tomorrow. This is—"

I turn on her.

"NO!"

My cheeks are on fire. "We're not doing ANYTHING, do you hear me? I don't . . . I just want them to go away. Especially that last one. We're . . . we're not giving them any more attention than they've . . ." My voice dies out.

"Okay. Okay." Abby's trying to calm me down. "But—"

I shake my head. I stick out my hand, little finger out. "Not a word! Pinky swear!"

The pinky swear has been our most solemn vow since forever. We've never broken one yet.

Abby hooks her pinky around mine.

"Fine. Pinky swear." She nods but doesn't look happy about it. "Ross. It was probably just a couple of people joking around, and it got out of control, y'know? One person trying to top the other, or . . . I don't know. And it went too far."

Suddenly, I can't breathe. I start spinning around looking for my stupid hat before I realize it's on my stupid head. I grab my backpack by one strap. Tears are coming, and I don't really want to be here when they arrive.

I pull open the bedroom door and hurry down the hallway.

"Ross!" Abby follows me. "Come on. Ross! Don't leave. Just stop."

I run down the stairs and pass Abby's mom in a blur. Then I'm outside. Across the lawn. Across the street. At the corner.

I see a few kids in costumes with their parents and do my best to ignore them. I stand on the corner, sucking in big gulps of the cool evening air. My heart is pounding like it wants to burst out of my chest.

I mean, I knew other students had been looking. Staring.

I'd seen kids pointing.

But I always assumed they were pulling for me on some level. For me to get better. To beat this thing. I mean . . . Is this all just some big joke to everyone at school?

I hear Abby calling my name, coming up behind me. I spin on her.

"Don't." I hold my hands up like a traffic cop. "I'm not mad at you, obviously, but I'm . . ." I mimic explosions coming out of my ears.

She nods. Looks at the ground. "I know. I get it. I'm mad too. And sad."

Two kids run by, laughing, with big pumpkin-shaped buckets.

I'm not sure whether to run, lie down, or spin around in circles. "I don't know how to . . . Who would make those?"

Abby looks up at me and shakes her head. Her eyes are watery. About to spill over. "I don't know, Ross. I really don't."

"Does . . . Someone would have to HATE me! Do people hate me?" I take a deep, shuddering breath. "I'm not DYING! Am I? Is there something I don't . . . Is Death waiting for me?"

Obviously, I know dying from this is a possibility— cancer does that—but I've gotten myself fairly convinced that I'm beating this thing. I even overheard my dad and Linda discussing "scary survival rates" one time, but it seemed like they were . . . Was I in denial? Do people in denial know they're in denial?

I suddenly feel like walls are closing in on me, even though I'm outside.

Abby steps closer, carefully, like she's approaching a wild animal. Then she moves to hug me, but I can't right now. I step back, give her arm a squeeze, and walk away.

I don't look back, and Abby doesn't follow.

It's a long walk to my house, but I'm okay with that. It's dark. There are a lot of people out—parents, kids, various ghouls—and I'm glad my face is hidden in shadows. I go back and forth between crying and fuming a few times. Sometimes both at the same time.

By the time I get home, I'm sniffling, but I've mostly pulled myself together. I go straight into the garage and grab my dad's stained old CD player from the work-bench. I open the top and take out *Journey's Greatest Hits*, whatever that is, and leave it on one of his work towels.

My dad and Linda look up as I stomp through the kitchen with the CD player, the power cord rattling across the floor behind me. I know my dad wants to ask why I'm home early, but the look on my face stops him. Or maybe Abby's mom called them.

In my room, I catch a glimpse of myself in the mirror—big dumb hat and all—and I really want to scream. I'm not sure who to be mad at, so I'm just mad. At the world. At myself for having stupid cancer.

I throw my hat at the wall and toss my backpack on the bed. I dig out Frank's CD and my earbuds. It's a minor miracle, but once I untangle them, they fit into the boom box's ancient jack.

Twenty seconds later, I'm on the bed, pillow over my head and awash in Ripe Sponge. I listen to that first song four times—my muscles slowly relaxing—before I move on to the second.

Then the third.

Fourteen songs about horny vampires and tragic love stories. Life on the road, teenage rebels, angry loners, and songs with screamed lyrics I mostly don't understand. Some of those are my favorites. The guitars seem to say what I'm feeling the best.

The guitars.

Stuttering rhythm lines. Wailing solos. Even the finger-picked ballads strike a nerve. Not to sound weird, but it's like a whole new language.

One I didn't know I needed until now.

By the time I fall asleep, I've listened to the entire mix at least three times.

12

THROCKTON

This seems like a good time to talk about how I met Dr. Throckton—the Man with All the Answers.

The morning after Dr. Popsicle told me they were going to take my eye and then blind me, I had no desire to get out of bed. None. But I did lie there looking at things in my room—toys, action figures—trying to memorize them. For later.

Like, if I went blind, would I remember what Homer Simpson looked like? Or would my memory of him slowly morph over time into some weird mutant Homer?

Then my eyes fell on the framed picture of my mom on the dresser. I went over to get it and lay there for half an hour trying to memorize every detail. Every curl in her hair. I couldn't forget. I wouldn't.

I mostly remember her from this picture. I was just about to turn five when she died, so one of the main things I remember is the feeling of lying next to her on the couch while she was sketching. She always smelled like fresh laundry. I could seriously go for some lying-next-to-Mom about now.

Then I went to my closet and pulled out a small leather photo album. My mom put it together for me before she died. It's full of photos of us together. Some with my dad too. Some are just of her.

The two of us at Kings Island, a person in a Scooby-Doo costume standing between us. Her feeding baby me, some kind of yellow stuff all over my face. One of my mom, her head back and her hair messed up, laughing so hard she has tears on her cheeks.

For some reason I try to only pull this out on rare occasions, like her birthday. It makes it more special.

I stared at her face in all those photos and wondered how she'd felt when *she* had cancer. It was like we had a new, unfortunate connection, and I may have missed her more right then than I ever have.

I found one of all three of us on the front steps. I look three or four. My mom's mouth was smiling, but I couldn't stop looking at her eyes. Were they smiling as well? Did she know she was sick when it was taken? Was there just a hint of fear in her eyes? Or worry? It was hard to say for sure, but there was something so warm and human there, I didn't want to stop looking for answers in them.

Near the back of the album, I've tucked a small note under the protective plastic. My mom wrote it—or wrote it for me—just after I turned four, when we were putting away our Christmas tree. (A fake tree. My dad's allergic.)

We found it the year after she died. Or at least my dad says we did. I don't really remember. It was in the bottom of the tree box in a red envelope.

> Dearest Future Ross—
> Hello! How was your year?
> I hope it was amazing!
> It's snowing the day I'm
> writing this. Do you remember?
> It's beautiful! I'm having
> Cocoa and it's so good.
> I just wanted to say Hi and
> remind you to have a
> great holiday! — Your Pal,
> Past Ross

My dad explained to me at some point that my mom sat down with me and wrote this. It was something she had done as a kid and was hoping I'd make a tradition: When you take the tree down, slip a note in there for your future self.

I've done it every year since.

He also told me my mom was in remission when she wrote this, so the cheery tone was real.

I lay there and read the note a few times until my eyes got all watery and then I carefully put it back in its protected spot.

Eventually, I got out of bed and put the photo album back. I spent a long time in the mirror trying to imagine myself with a fake eye. I mean, I already felt weird with just a hat and a bald spot. How was I going to . . . Was I gonna look like the Phantom of the Opera? Would I scare small children?

I made a mental note to look up facial prosthetics, but I wasn't exactly rushing to the computer. I was pretty sure I wouldn't like what I saw.

My dad and Linda were at the kitchen table. Linda was next to my dad, rubbing his back as they sat and read their Kindles. Probably reading the books Dr. Popsicle recommended. When I walked in, they quickly set them aside and gave me their full, concerned attention.

"Hey, bud." My dad jumped up, wiping his eyes and looking away. For the first time, I realized he was at least as scared as I was.

"Want some breakfast? I can make hole-in-ones! Or scrambled?"

I shook my head, looking around the kitchen. Again, I was memorizing. I couldn't stop. We'd lived in this house since before I could remember—if I looked over at that frog-shaped cookie jar, was there a chance it would be the last time I'd see it?

"I'm not really hungry." The thought of eggs made me feel carsick.

He nodded. "Okay. Sure. Wanna go do something? You name it."

"I don't think . . . Is it okay if I just go down and play a video game?"

"Absolutely." He gave me a weak smile. "You do you. I have some people that should be calling me back. We may take you for a second opinion. To another doctor. Or . . ."

Linda reached over and rubbed my arm. "You just go take it easy, okay? Yell up if you want me to bring you anything." She smiled. "Anything."

I went to the basement but didn't put on a game. I just ended up lying on my back. Thinking. Zoning out. I may have drifted in and out of sleep a couple of times.

At some point I got up and tried navigating around the furniture with my eyes closed. A Blindness Test Run. The more I felt my way around, the more the panic tightened up in my chest.

That lasted until I racked myself pretty good on a bar stool.

That was enough practice for the day, so I went into *Annihilation: Moon* zone.

A little before noon, my dad's phone rang, and a few minutes later I heard the door to the basement open.

My dad came down the steps quickly, and when I turned, I saw something like hope on his face. He was still holding the phone.

"Who was that?" I asked, not really expecting much.

My dad took a shuddery, deep breath. "That was Dr. Sheffler. He has someone we need to talk with."

At 3:18 that afternoon, I met Dr. Throckton. As he came into the room, I spotted a partially eaten Pop-Tart sticking out of his coat pocket.

LOOKED LIKE BROWN SUGAR CINNAMON

He was carrying a clipboard, a couple of folders, and a Scrabble mug dripping coffee. His hair was messed up—which gave him a mad scientist vibe—but when he introduced himself, he was all business.

He shook my hand first. "You must be Ross. Thank you for coming to see me." He looked over at my dad and

Linda. "I'm glad Dr. Sheffler insisted we meet. And thank you for having the scans sent over." Back to me. "Ross, you have a *very* interesting case."

Dr. Throckton was apparently some sort of miracle worker with proton radiotherapy. I was really hoping so, at this point.

He foot-hooked his stool over in that effortless way they must teach in med school. Rolled over to a computer and waggled the mouse to wake up the screen. It filled with a black-and-white scan of a brain. My brain. And my eyeballs. My tumor.

My dad couldn't take the suspense. "So do you think you can help?"

"Oh, yeah." Throckton took a sip of his coffee. "I can save Ross's eye."

We all sat there for a second.

"You mean the good eye? Or the other one? I don't . . ."

He smiled. "I mean both of 'em." Then he turned to me. "Don't let them take your eye, Ross."

Dr. Throckton shot immediately to the position of Favorite Person Ever for All Time and earned the nickname the Man with All the Answers. My dad and I still call him that.

Then he began to talk. And explain. And within five minutes, I knew I was in a room with the smartest person I'd ever met. He took us through the scans—little cross sections of my brain and eyes and the tumor—and talked about them until they made sense. He explained all about proton radiotherapy in a way that made me feel smarter just hearing it. It turns out it's different from traditional radiation. With protons, they can zap just the things they want to zap, and not the stuff they don't. Like my "good" eye.

"Now, Ross, you *will* lose the sight in your right eye. But we won't remove it. Or the orbit."

I thought about that for a few seconds. I could deal with that. Especially given the alternative.

"I'm okay with one blind eye, I guess."

Throckton nodded. "I thought you would be. Given the alternative."

He looked relieved that I'd taken it so well. "And it'll take a while for the vision in that eye to go. It's not an instant thing."

"Okay. But not in the good eye."

He nodded. "Not the good eye. We'll protect that one with our life."

And just like that, we had a new plan.

Have surgery. (A much less severe one that left my eye intact.)

Recover.

Get zapped a couple months later.

I walked out of there like a boss. I was going to go through a difficult surgery and eight weeks of radiation and lose the sight in one of my eyes ... and yet I felt like a million bucks.

MILLION-DOLLAR BATPIG

13

PLAY THAT FUNKY MUSIC

The day after the Bad Halloween—or *the Night of the Memes*—is a Saturday, and my radiation is scheduled for nine a.m. I'm awake and dressed by eight thirty, waiting on the stairs for my dad. He doesn't ask what happened the night before, but I feel the curiosity coming off him in waves.

My mind is surprisingly focused, given how incredibly upset I was the night before.

The waiting room is empty, so I sit with my jaw set and listen to the aquariums bubble for what feels like forever. When I finally hear the electric doors open, I'm off the couch moving. Frank comes through, smiling.

"Ross! Did you—"

I cut him off. "Can you teach me guitar?"

He stops, his smile shifting. He looks off for a second, thinking.

"Umm . . . I suppose so? I mean . . . I've never taught anyone . . . but I could try." He squints at me, puzzled. "What's up? You okay?"

I waggle my head and my hand. "Not really. No. Also, I don't have a guitar."

Frank nods for a few seconds. "That's okay. I've got you covered."

"So, okay." I breathe. Crack a couple knuckles. It feels like blood is flowing back into my body for the first time since Abby told me about the memes.

"So, okay." He's still nodding. Small, thoughtful nods. "C'mon."

After my treatment, I text my dad, so he can come inside and talk with Frank.

The niceties out of the way, I get straight to business. I put on my most serious face. "Dad, I've asked Frank to teach me guitar."

My dad looks back and forth at us, his eyebrows up. "I . . . Guitar? Okay . . . You give guitar lessons?"

"Nope. Never even thought about it." Frank shakes his head. "But I play. A lot. And I guess I'm willing to give the teaching part a try. I mean, I'll have to check that it's okay with the bosses here, but . . . yeah."

My dad looks back at me, caught off guard. Even though Abby's been after me to take up an instrument for a couple of years, I've never shown the slightest interest. And I hated every second when we had to play the recorder in fifth grade.

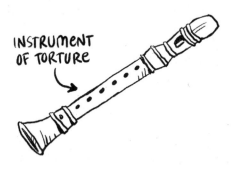

INSTRUMENT
OF TORTURE

We end up sitting in the waiting room while my dad and Frank sip coffee, discussing how this would work. I can tell my dad is unsure about this bearded, shaggy-haired tech at first, but Frank gets him laughing a few times—like I knew he would—and I can see my dad relax. Frank suggests we both come by his house the next day after Ripe Sponge gets done with their practice.

"Ripe Sponge?"

Frank gives his head a sad shake and holds up a hand. "Yeah, That's . . . Good band, horrible name. It's a long story."

"Fair enough." My dad looks over at me. "What are these lessons going to cost?" He seems more amused than concerned.

Frank finishes a sip and swallows quickly. "No, no. Let's try a couple first. On me. I may very well be terrible at this. But if not, we'll figure something out."

And just like that, it's settled.

That night Abby has some big dinner with her family planned. Her dad got them reservations at Abby's favorite place. (An old steak place called Janko's Little Zagreb, with steaks the size of a hubcap. I mentioned she's not a dainty eater.) Her dad said they're having a Family Meeting. Whatever that means.

We text a couple of times when they're on their way to Janko's, mostly about how *Destroy All Monsters* is on at eleven on some obscure channel. She agrees to text me after dinner.

I hang out in my room and listen to the mix, trying to run through the faces of all the kids in my school. Who'd be the type to make those memes?

I don't have many suspects, but one face keeps popping into my mind.

Jimmy (aka Mr. Spit).

If there's a kid with a legendary mean streak in our school, that's the guy.

I must fall asleep, because at some point I'm jolted awake by my phone buzzing. It's Abby, which is really weird. She communicates by text almost exclusively. Occasionally she'll FaceTime, but she literally never uses her phone as a phone. So something is off.

I answer, and the first thing I hear is a loud, snotty sniff on the other end. I think she's crying, and my heart stops.

"Abby? What's wrong?"

She sniffs a couple more times and blows her nose. "Rossss."

Something isn't good.

"I . . . I have news. Bad news, okay?"

I bolt upright in bed. "Is everybody okay?"

"Yeah, it's not like that." As she speaks, I realize she isn't crying quite as hard as I thought, but it sounds like she was recently. "Do . . . do you remember my dad was talking with his brother? About that job in Minnesota, working with him?"

Now I see the punch coming, in slow motion, but there's nothing I can do to stop it.

I take as deep a breath as my lungs will let me. "Yeah."

"He's, um . . . he's taking it. We're moving. To Saint Paul. Where my uncle's family is." She caps it with a little sad intake of air.

I'm stunned.

Her dad has talked, off and on, about going to work with his brother—some kind of software business that is doing really well—but it's always just been dinner table chatter. Not something that might actually happen.

I start to speak, and it's hard to get words around the rock that's suddenly stuck in my throat. "Wh-when?"

She sniffs. "Christmas break. Like, as soon as we're done with school. They put it off till then for me and school, or else we'd be going now."

"Christmas break? That's, like, two months from now!"

She lets out a small "Yep" and I let that sink in.

"Wait. Seriously? This isn't one of your—"

"Seriously." She cuts me off. "Pinky swear, unfortunately."

I scoot back so I can lean against the headboard. I'm looking around my room, searching for the right thing to say.

"I don't. Want that." It sounds stupid and awkward as it comes out.

Abby lets out a sad little sound. Like a sigh mixed with a groan. "I know. I don't either."

Am I gonna barf? I may barf. A horrifying thought occurs to me. "Oh, man. First Isaac. Now you. I'm gonna have to make new friends."

She laughs, kind of. "Right? Me too. I'll be going to my cousin's school, but still."

Abby has a cousin in St. Paul her same age named April. Super popular. Cheerleader. All that.

"You'll be fine. You've got April and all her friends."

Abby sighs. "April's a twit. You've met her."

She's right. April is a twit.

"Also, don't lump me with Isaac." Another sniff. I can tell her nose is almost stuffed shut. "This move isn't my choice."

"Sorry."

We sit in total silence for a couple of minutes, which is a long time in phone silence. The rest of my public-school career yawns out in front of me like a huge, best-friendless question mark. Abby's too.

"Wow." It doesn't even sound like my voice.

"Yeah, wow. So . . . I guess, let's just . . . We'll talk about it more . . . soon. I guess. Tomorrow."

"Okay." I run a hand through my hair. "Yeah. We'll sleep on it and . . . I don't know. Talk about it tomorrow. Or something."

"'Kay." Her voice sounds so small for Abby.

"Sorry about last night. I freaked out."

"No. I get it. Good night, Ross." Then she's gone.

I sit there staring off into space for maybe twenty minutes, then decide to put Frank's mix CD back on.

It helps.

Sort of.

14

GENTLEMEN, START YOUR GUITARS

I tell my dad and Linda about the Petersons' moving over breakfast, and my dad is genuinely shocked. It's not like he and Abby's dad are best friends, but they play tennis with a group of guys sometimes.

"Wow. I knew he'd talked about it, but . . ." Then his eyes change, and he looks back at me. "Buddy. I'm so sorry."

Linda, who's been carefully dusting and straightening one of my mom's landscape paintings—she does that a lot—comes over to give me a hug and a kiss on the top of my head. "Oh, honey. Are you okay? I had a good friend move away my sophomore year of high school. It's so hard."

I look up at her. "Are you still good friends with her?"

She looks like she's sorry she brought it up. "Yeah. I

mean we . . . Yeah. We send each other cards over the holidays."

She sits down and awkwardly adjusts the spider decoration in the middle of the kitchen table. No one's taken the Halloween decorations down yet, but skulls and ghouls seem appropriate for my mood.

It turns out Frank doesn't live too far from us. Only a few miles or so, but his area has a lot of houses for IU students. The lawns aren't really taken care of—at all— and there are a lot of old couches and lawn chairs on the front porches. The house next to his has a faded Bud Lite WELCOME RACE FANS banner hanging from the front porch railing.

My dad pulls up slowly, squinting at Frank's house. It's a dark, ugly brown, and it's set back from the road under several big trees—all of which makes it seem a little less than inviting.

"M'kay. It's not *too* bad. It reminds me of a house I shared after college. Let's go check it out." My dad's talking slow, like he's convincing himself this is a good idea.

There's a gaping hole in my stomach—I can't stop thinking about Abby's move—but I hop out before he can change his mind.

I try to keep him distracted as we make our way up the gravel driveway. "I think we had a pool just like that one when I was little, didn't we?" There's a broken plastic kiddie pool in the yard on the other side. A couple of faded cans are floating in murky water at the bottom.

"Yeah..." He looks like he's waiting for someone to jump out of the bushes and corrupt me. "Yeah, we did..."

Frank comes out onto the porch, screen door squeaking. He's wearing a black button-down shirt and jeans, and I realize I've never seen him in anything but scrubs. It's weird.

"Welcome, Ross! Welcome, Ross's dad!" He raises a can of Diet Coke in salute. "The band just left, so we actually have the place to ourselves for once. Come on in, and I'll show you the Palace."

When we step in, I'm actually impressed. Most of the furniture is fake black leather and showing signs of serious wear, but it's clean, and the house smells okay. There's a scented candle lit in the middle of an old trunk that's being used as a coffee table. Some of the area rugs have seen better days, but it looks like the hardwood floors have been swept.

The back wall is made up of bookshelves overflowing with vinyl albums and stack after stack of cassettes.

I point at them. "You know you could put all of that on an MP3 player that'd fit in your pocket."

Frank rolls his eyes. "I don't like my music broken down into ones and zeros. I allow the occasional CD, but only under protest." He looks over at my dad, who smiles and gives a that-makes-sense nod.

"I get that. I like a nice hiss and pop. Adds character."

Frank raises his eyebrows at me. "See? Your dad gets it."

In front of the dining room table are two acoustic guitars, propped on metal stands, like they're waiting for us.

"So." Frank waves a hand around. "This is where the magic happens, as they say on the music television." I don't know what that means, but it makes my dad laugh. "You ready to have sore fingers, Ross?"

I look at him, unsure how to respond. He walks over and grabs the older-looking guitar. "Trust me. They're gonna hurt. For a while. But you'll build up calluses." He holds out the guitar.

I don't think I've ever held one. I take it and feel its weight. He motions for me to put the strap over my head. I do, and everything about it feels right. Not to be a *total* dweeb, but I can't help but think of Luke holding a lightsaber for the first time.

Okay. Yeah. I regret saying the lightsaber thing now.

"That's the guitar I sto . . . liberated from my cousin . . . way, way back. I taught myself on it. It's a solid guitar. A Yamaha."

My dad is smiling. "Your cousin didn't want it back?"

Frank sets his can down on a faded Rolling Rock coaster. "Nah. He caught the hunting bug that year and never looked back. He'd won it in a school raffle or something, anyway. Never even tuned it."

My dad nods, giving one last look around.

"Okay. All right. So . . . I'll get out of here and leave you guys to it?" He pulls his keys out of his jacket, apparently convinced Frank's house isn't a danger zone. "I'll be back in an hour."

We agree, and he heads out. Frank waits until the

screen door slaps shut behind him and claps his hands together.

"All right, all right, all right!" He points at the fridge. "Beer?"

I must look shocked, 'cause he laughs. "I'm kidding, Ross. Just a little icebreaker. Now, go sit in that chair. Let's do some guitaring."

15

STUPID FINGERS

So . . . it turns out playing guitar is really hard.

I mean, I figured I wouldn't be laying down wailing guitar solos the first night or anything, but I also didn't expect to be so truly disappointed in my idiot fingers.

Frank starts the lesson with a C chord. Well . . . first he shows me how to play a single note. We're starting from scratch here.

"When you hold that down here and pluck it? That's a note. Let's not worry about *which* note yet. Try a couple."

Then he explains that a chord is a collection of notes played together. Like, you hold a few strings down in different places and then strum with the other hand, and together they make a whole new sound.

He shows me where to put the fingers of my left hand on the neck of the guitar to make a C chord.

If you do it right, it looks all cool and easy. But that's not what happens.

My fingers freak out and push down strings they aren't supposed to and just misbehave in general.

Within three minutes, I'm majorly frustrated. Like, nose-itchingly frustrated.

But I keep trying, and trying . . . and finally, on maybe the eighteen hundredth try, I get it right.

"THERE! YES!" Frank looks genuinely excited. "Hold that. Remember how it feels." I run the thumb of my right hand over the strings, and the sound is amazing. It feels like it resonates in my bones. I strum it a few more times and can't believe I'm making that sound happen.

"No way! That's awesome!"

Then he shows me the right way to hold a pick and

how to use it with the strumming hand, and I keep play-ing that C over and over and over. Frank grabs his guitar and shows me an easy strumming pattern.

Once I have a rhythm going, he kicks his feet up on the trunk, grinning.

"Look at you! You're playing guitar!"

I can't help but smile, playing that same chord over and over and over.

And that's when Darth Vader walks in the front door.

Jimmy freakin' Jenkins.

My laugh dies in my throat as Jimmy notices me. He freezes too—even his gum chomping stops. The back of my neck is instantly on fire. I haven't seen him since the whole meme thing, and right now he's the only person on my list of suspects.

"What the..." Jimmy's eyebrows furrow. He's as confused as I am. The screen door keeps squeaking as his body blocks it from closing all the way. "What are you doing here, Maloy?"

I look over at Frank, who's looking back and forth at us. "You guys know each other?"

"Yeah." I mutter. "We ... school ..."

Frank starts nodding. "Oh, right! Duh. That makes sense."

I look at him. "It *does*?"

Frank laughs. "Jimmy's cousin is my drummer. Denny. He lives here. Well, he pays rent here, but he's not around much lately." He looks back to Jimmy. "Denny took off a while ago. I think he went to Jana's place."

Jimmy hasn't moved. "This is friggin' weird. How do you guys . . . How do you know Ross?"

"I know Ross from the proton center. Where I work?" Frank sits back. "Radiation?"

Jimmy stares. "I didn't know you . . . What are you, a doctor or somethin'?"

"I'm a radiation tech, Jimmy. You know that. We've talked about it. Now, get out of here. We've got a serious lesson going on. I'm on the clock." Then he stands there rubbing at the half 'stache on his upper lip. "So weird." Then he gives me a quick scowl and backs out. "Whatever." The screen door squawks and slaps shut as he lumbers down the front deck stairs.

I look over at Frank. "You know *JIMMY*?"

"Yeah, he lives a few blocks over. Comes over here sometimes to hang out with Denny. Or maybe it's just to get out of his house." He gets up and walks to the kitchen.

He looks back and winces, like he's debating how to say something. "Maybe not a stellar home situation for Jimmy, as you might imagine. His mom's a bit of a . . ." He doesn't finish the sentence. Waves it off. "Never mind."

He grabs another Diet Coke out of the fridge—holds one up for me, but I shake my head. I'm trying to find the perfect words to eloquently explain how I'm feeling. Then I find them.

"Jimmy's a total %$#&@!"

Frank pauses for half a second at my choice of words, then shuffles over and sits back down. "Probably." He thinks about it for a second. "But he's pretty harmless. Just kind of a mess, from what I can tell. So is Denny, if I'm being honest—but he's a really good drummer." He takes a long drink, then gestures at the guitar. "Okay. Let's get going."

I look down, having completely forgotten the guitar around my neck.

Frank holds his hand up and waggles his fingers. "Come on. Find your C again."

I try, but I'm rattled.

It takes me a while to stop picturing Jimmy hunched over some grungy little computer making Cowboy Cancer memes. I think about mentioning them to Frank but decide not to.

Eventually, my dumb fingers start working again and I get a decent C going. Frank has me let go with my fingers, then find the spot again. And again. And again, until I can do it quicker and quicker. Until it feels natural.

I mean, relatively natural.

When the hour is almost up, Frank tells me I can take a guitar home so I can practice. Then he goes in the back and comes out with a beat-up old guitar case. It has band stickers all over it and RiPE SPoNgE stenciled down one side in sloppy orange spray paint.

It may be the coolest thing I've ever seen.

My dad shows up promptly at five, waiting out front. I stand up and thank Frank. "You're a good coach, Coach. Not that I have any other ones to compare you to."

"Well. Ya done good, child." He holds out a fist, and

I bump it. "But seriously, go home and work at it. Like, get crazy working at it. Your fingers are gonna hate you, but that's how you get better." He holds the screen door open for me. "I want to see deep, painful dents in your tips from the strings."

"Gotcha. Fingertip dents. I'm on it. See you soon." I'm out the door when I remember something. I hand him a folded-up piece of paper out of my back pocket. It's the flyer Sarah gave me about the talent show.

"I realize this thing's only, like, six or seven weeks away, but I thought maybe . . . I don't know . . . Do you think by then I could . . ."

Frank reads it, chewing his bottom lip. "I don't see why not. It depends on you, really." He looks at me for a moment, thinking. "You may get tired from the treatments, you know. But if you think you're feeling okay . . ." He hands the flyer back. "Let's reassess in a couple of weeks."

"Yeah. Yeah, that's good. It was just a thought." I turn and start down the steps.

"Wait a second." I can hear Frank is smiling, even without looking back. "This whole guitar thing isn't all just to impress some girl, is it?"

I keep walking and yell over my shoulder, "Not entirely!"

Frank laughs, and I hear the screen door whack shut.

Walking down that weed-infested gravel driveway with a battered guitar case hanging at the end of my arm—even as I look around nervously for Jimmy to jump out and throttle me—I feel the best I have in weeks.

16

SORE FINGERS

Frank told me to "Play it till my fingers bleed." It turns out it's a reference to some song I don't know, but when I get home, that's exactly what I do.

Actually, the bleeding fingers come later. That first night they just throb and ache so bad I think they're going to pop. It feels like the strings—especially the thicker, copper ones—hate my fingers and are trying to cut them through to the bone.

But I don't want to stop. I sit there on my bed with some of Frank's song books and my dad's CD player and try to figure out some of the chords.

It's HARD. At times I think I'm guitar-tab dyslexic and want to throw the book across the room—but then I lie back, take a few deep breaths, and try again. And again. And again.

Abby keeps texting, but I'm putting off seeing her for some reason. I know that's dumb, but part of me is pretty sure I'm going to bawl like a baby as soon as I see her face and we start talking about the move. I have this picture of us collapsing into a big gooey pile of blubbering sadness, and I'm not ready for that.

But she's relentless. She wants to see a movie. She has questions about some homework. She can't remember the punch line to some dumb joke.

The texts keep coming.

I continue to avoid her—maybe I secretly want to wait until I become a guitar expert and surprise her—which is a great plan for a couple of hours, until my bedroom door swings open.

It's Abby, of course.

She looks around, taking in the whole scene. There are open guitar tab books on the bed next to some spilled Cheetos. CDs and their cases are all over the place. "Sounds of Silence" is playing on the CD player.

I blush like she caught me playing with Barbies. I was

going to tell her about the guitar stuff, obviously. I just hadn't yet.

"So . . ." She walks in and picks up the Simon and Garfunkel book. "You've decided to become a youth minister?"

I take the book from her. "Not exactly."

"Camp counselor? Soft rock superstar?"

"Nope. I'm just . . . playing a little guitar."

She picks up a plastic pick. "M'kay. So, Ross . . . You *are* Ross, right?" She makes an exaggerated face like we've never met. "When did you become a musician?"

I look around at the CDs. The books. "Yesterday?"

"Yesterday." Nodding. "Gotcha." She walks over and plops into a chair. "I came over to whine to you about the move, but this is SO much more interesting." She waves a hand at the whole scene. "I can whine tomorrow. Fill me in."

I take a deep breath and tell her all of it. I tell her about Frank, and Frank's mix. I don't get all crazy with all that stuff about how the music feels like a "language I never knew I needed," but I tell her I really, really liked it. I tell her about the lesson and about Jimmy.

She's staring. "Listen to me. You're not gonna start hanging out with Jimmy when I leave, are you? Start spitting in bottles?"

"Oh, trust me. I'm pretty sure Jimmy made those . . . photo things." I tip my head back and apply some eye drops. I'm like the LeBron James of putting in eye drops these days. "It was all I could do not to throw a chair at him."

Abby kicks off her neon orange high-tops. "So, okay. Play me something. This is exciting!"

"Oh!" The idea shakes me enough that I laugh. "God, no!" I slip the strap over my head and prop the guitar carefully against the side of the bed. "I barely know how to hold the thing at this point."

"I heard you from the hallway, dingus, and it actually sounded halfway okay. I mean, considering I've never seen you in the same room as a guitar." She has her lip balm out. "So, were you gonna tell me at some point?"

I'm stacking the books and putting CDs back in their cases. "Yeah. I was just . . . I don't know . . . You've got a lot going on and all, with the move . . ."

"Yeah." She sighs. "That." She grabs a Transformer off of my bookshelf. "I didn't do much but stare at a wall today. And, I mean, you've got that plus the whole memes mess."

I put a hand up. "Is there some other word we can use? I hate that word, *meme*." I drop the pick into a little compartment in the open guitar case. "*Meme*."

Abby laughs. "It is kind of stupid . . . *Meme*."

"*Meeeme*." I say it like the word itself is disgusting.

Then she sings it. "Meme-meme-meme-meme!"

"So stupid." I laugh. "Why *meme*? Why not a *flerb* or a *guanch*?"

"Actually, I think I read it's from the Greek word for 'imitating.'"

I glare at her. "I wasn't really asking, nerd." Then I stand up. "You want a Coke? I could use a Coke."

Abby slips her lip balm into a pocket of her jeans. "I'd take a Coke. But don't think I'm leaving until you play me something." She's smiling, but she looks serious. "Then I'm gonna dig deep and psychoanalyze this whole New Ross thing. Gonna get all Dr. Phil on you."

She puts her chin on both of her fists and gives me her exaggerated attention. "You *fascinate* me, Ross Maloy."

"Okay," I say, walking out. "When you figure me all out, can you fill me in as well?"

She only stays for an hour—I think she can tell I want to get back to practicing. We laugh and mess around on our phones for a while. Then, after she blasts me with over-the-top Abby encouragement to play at the talent show, I give in and play a couple of chords for her.

But only a couple.

17

THE PIT

So, there was another Bad Day.

It was about a month after my surgery. Beginning of September, a few weeks into the school year. A few weeks before I started radiation. My eye was pretty well healed, but they had to wait a while before they could put the little BBs in my head so the beam would zap the right spot. (What I now refer to as the Dime Slot procedure.) So I didn't have my dime slot yet.

I was cleaning my room, and it was a true mess. Linda was cooking downstairs. My dad wasn't home yet. It was dark out.

I was going through a pile of stuff on my side table when I came to an issue of the Walking Dead comic. No big deal, but for some reason that word, *Dead*, stuck in my head.

Then I remembered what Dr. Throckton had said when he looked at my post-surgery scans. That with any luck it wouldn't come back. Like, in my lungs or somewhere. Because if it did, there was nothing they could do for this particular type of tumor. He didn't think that was likely, but it was a possibility.

Back at that time, when he told me that, I did something really weird. I just brushed it off. Pushed it out of my thoughts. I blocked it out and decided not to dwell on it.

Until that night in my room—straightening up with the dark of the night creeping in—when that conversation jumped out of my brain like the boogeyman.

I could *die*.

That was obviously an option all along—and I knew it—but in that moment, in that gloomy room, for some unknown reason . . . it finally sunk in.

Like, *really* sunk in.

And it sunk in hard.

I felt the floor tip under me. I don't mean that in a fancy-pants, writing way. I mean it felt like *the floor actually tipped under my feet*—severely—and then dropped away.

Like there was nothing beneath me to catch me.

It was the weirdest feeling. Like there was an endless

black space under me, and I was dangling there like Wile E. Coyote in the worst, scariest cartoon ever.

I collapsed down to my knees next to the bed.

And then I was crying. Out of one eye, of course— 'cause I don't have a stupid lacrimal gland on the right side anymore—which just made me feel even worse.

One-eyed crying.

Not even crying. Bawling, maybe. Or, one time I heard the word *keening* means crying super hard, but when I looked it up, it means crying for a lost loved one. So I guess I keened? Maybe I was keening for myself, as weird as that sounds. Crying at the very real, scary knowledge that I might not live through this. What if the cancer came back and they couldn't help me?

I could be gone, and life would just . . . go on. My friends would go to high school. And college. New Star Wars movies would come out. Just without me there to see them. Like I never even happened . . .

My dad would be wrecked. First his wife and now his kid?

Fortunately, Linda had KZAQ on in the kitchen, so she didn't hear me. I curled up in a ball, and it came out of me like a faucet.

For maybe ten minutes.

Then I was left sniffling and catching my breath on

the floor. Wiped out. Drained like a burst water balloon. Crying that hard is like running a marathon.

That's when Linda walked by the room. She caught a glimpse of me crumpled there and Freaked Out.

"ROSS!" She came flying in fast and grabbed me before I could react. "Are you okay? What's wrong?"

I turned and sat up as fast as I could so she'd know I wasn't dead, but she was already upset. There were tears in her eyes as she swept me into a tight hug.

"OH! Oh, Ross. Don't do that to me! What happened?"

I used my sleeve to wipe my eyes and running nose. (Gross, but necessary.)

"I'm okay. I am. I just had a thing. A moment."

She kissed the top of my head and rested her cheek there for a bit, and I had a flash memory of my mom doing that to me when I was sick, or just sad. Then she held me out a bit so she could see my swollen eyes. Wiped her cheeks, which were wet as well now.

"Just . . . bad thoughts?"

I nodded. "Really bad."

She leaned back against the side of my bed but held on to my arm. Caught her breath. "You . . . Do you wanna talk about it?"

I sat for a minute staring at the stuff I'd knocked off the side table on my way down.

"I just started thinking about . . . the worst-case scenario."

She nodded and chewed her lip. "Oh, boy. You're fine, Ross. We got this. But I suppose that'll creep into your head from time to time."

I pulled in a huge sniff—my nose was still running—and she went on.

"Maybe when that happens, you try to actively think of something else instead. 'Cause thinking about it doesn't do you any good. So you go draw or watch one of your monster movies or something."

"So, live in denial?" It was a serious question.

She laughed. "No. Not denial. Just try not to dwell on it."

"Well . . ." I slid over so I was sitting next to her. "I wasn't really dwelling. This came on like a sneak attack. I was fine and then it kind of pounced out of my brain, like . . . Boom."

She nodded. "Yeah. Thoughts'll do that sometimes."

We sat there for a while, listening to the radio drifting up from the kitchen. A Maroon 5 song and then something by Pink.

At some point I leaned against her, my face against her shoulder. And then we just kept sitting there, for a good while.

The storm had passed.

18

BACK TO SCHOOL
(OR HOW TO MAKE FRIENDS
AND INFLUENCE PEOPLE)

On Monday, I'm on high alert. From the moment I step through the doors, every kid with a phone is now a meme suspect. Jimmy is still at the top of my list, but there's no way to be 100 percent sure.

I've heard that animals, when backed into a corner, have this fight-or-flight response. Will they stand their ground and get all aggressive, or do they head for the hills? My fight/flight response is at war in my head as I pass the trophy cases by the front offices. Part of me wants to be literally anywhere but here, but another part wants to pin every single kid in the halls against a locker until they tell me the truth.

Danny Hill—a kid whose birthday parties I went to up until second grade—comes around the corner and sees me and my hat. He hooks his thumbs in his armpits like he has suspenders on.

"Git 'er done, cowpoke!"

I brush past him, giving him a look that melts his smile. I'm almost around the corner when I spin back around.

He's looking back too. "Hey, sorry, Ross. I was just—"

"Did you see the memes, Danny?" I try not to sound too angry or upset, but my voice cracks to where I sound a little unhinged.

"What memes?"

I study his face. "Cancer Cowboy? Death? You didn't see those?"

Danny puts his hands up. "I . . . Whoa . . . I was just joking around with the cowpoke thing."

"Okay . . ." I let my shoulders fall. "Okay." I'm still not sure I believe him, but there's really nothing I can do to prove it. "It's . . . it's just been . . . Sorry." I move on.

In Ms. Bayer's class, I'm hyperaware of everyone around me. How they look at me.

And I get looks. It's hard not to start yelling questions at every person that glances my way.

I'm mulling it over and getting more and more irritated when Jimmy drops into his seat beside me.

"Well, well! If it ain't Mr. Geee-tar Man." Only he stretches *guitar* out, dripping with sarcasm. He's chomping on his gum, his open spit jar in hand, and the area around his mouth is glistening in a way that makes me feel queasy. "You gonna favor us with a tune, Guitar Man? Gonna play us a little ditty?" He's talking loud enough for the whole class to hear. Sarah turns her head just enough that I can tell she's listening. And she's not the only one. The room is all ears.

I feel steam boiling up in my head as I picture that stupid cartoon of Death with my name on it. Death, waiting for me.

Jimmy shakes his head as he chomps away like a cow. Looks around at the class. "Little Rossy thinks he's some kinda fancy musician. Maybe if we're really good, he'll—"

Something snaps inside my head.

With one quick move, I whip my Language Arts book at Jimmy. It hits him hard in the neck. A ball of gum the size of a softball flies out of his mouth with an audible *phoont*. His eyes go wide, and he makes a loud noise like *GACK!* The bottle falls from his hands and clacks loudly on the ground, spilling spit everywhere.

"Shut up, Jimmy! Shut your face!" I'm leaning across the aisle, whisper-shouting at him. "Did you make those photos? I know it was you, you big stupid—"

"Guh! Puh!" Jimmy's holding his neck and sputtering. He goes from shock to fury. "OH, YOU'RE DEAD! YOU JUST PUNCHED YOUR TICKET, DORK!"

He makes no effort to keep his voice down. He lunges across the aisle and—with a hand the size of an oven mitt—swats the back of my head, sending my hat flying. Then he smashes the side of my face and pulls me toward him. I'm seeing stars as I kick out and connect with the side of his desk.

I can't stop. I keep kicking as I slide out of my chair,

my sweatshirt hiking up under my arms. Jimmy lunges, grabs a handful of fabric. I kick again and catch him hard in the armpit.

"STOP IT! STOP IT, YOU TWO! JIMMY!"

It's Ms. Bayer, suddenly there. She jumps between us and throws her weight into Jimmy, pushing him away from me. Then she slips in his spit and gum and goes down.

Hard.

Jimmy lunges around her and connects with a ham-sized fist on my upper lip and my nose.

Ms. Bayer is trying to get up, and I see that she's landed on the gum. It's stretching between the tiles and her backside as she struggles.

I can feel the emotions climbing my throat like a lump. Before I can swallow them, they burst out of my eyes, and I'm hunched over, covering my face and trying to stop a handful of really embarrassing sobs. The kids around us have jumped up and scattered. Their faces look like they've just witnessed a murder.

The smell of grape gum spit is in my nose as I realize some of it got on my jeans. My leg is wet.

Somehow, I still have enough vanity in me to be worrying about my hat head.

I'm curled up against something, and I look up. I'm pinned up against Sarah Kennedy's leg. I sort of have her trapped there. Her eyes are big, and she looks freaked out and disgusted—and she's desperately trying to get her leg out from beside me.

But I can't stop the crying. Full-on snot-slinging crying, like it's never going to stop. I look around and see a handful of my classmates looking at me like an alien.

"Stop it!" My voice cracks and bubbles. "Quit looking at me!" I cover my face and realize I've seen that look on people's faces before. In fifth grade when Stan Hardin wet his pants because Ms. Falsey wouldn't give him a bathroom pass.

I know what that look is.

It's pity.

And that's when I officially wish I could crawl under the floor tiles and die.

19

HAULED IN

Jimmy and I are sitting at opposite ends of the long wooden bench outside the principal's office. We look like mismatched bookends. The school nurse has given us each an ice pack—mine for my lip and Jimmy's for his throat—and we're not looking at each other. We can hear Ms. Bayer's excited rambling coming from the office.

". . . Not on MY watch. No way, no sir. Never seen anything the likes of this in all of my sixteen years teaching these little . . ."

"I know you made those memes." I mumble it through gritted teeth.

Jimmy turns slowly. "What the crap are you talking about?" Only he doesn't censor himself.

This sets me off again.

"*Cancer Cowboy?* Me farting through a hospital gown? Does that ring a bell? You must be really proud, 'cause it seems like everybody's seen 'em! They're all the rage in the textiverse."

Jimmy glares at me. It's only been a few minutes since the Rumble in the Classroom, and now, feeling the heat of his stare, I wonder if we might start fighting again right here. "Do I look like I have a phone, moron? Do I? You think I'm on any 'textiverse'?"

"YOU JUST CALLED ME CANCER COWBOY ON FRIDAY! What is that, a coincidence?"

Jimmy's eyebrows furrow as he adjusts his ice pack. "I didn't call you Cancer Cowboy! I just said Cowboy. And it wasn't a big stretch—YOU WERE WEARING A FRIGGIN' COWBOY HAT! YOU STILL ARE!"

"Whatever." I turn back away. "I don't believe you." He has a point, but I'm still so mad I could scream.

"Whatever."

"Whatever."

The door opens, and Ms. Bayer sails by without even looking at us. Then Principal Kingsley is there. He's a big, balding guy. He doesn't look happy.

"Gentlemen." Actually, he looks more tired than anything. "Step in here. Let's talk."

Principal Kingsley's office is small and seems more so from all of the sports memorabilia on every available wall and surface. It's also about five degrees warmer than it needs to be.

He sits back and lets us each tell our side of the story. Once I mention the memes, he's more interested in those than the actual fight.

"So, Jimmy. You didn't make any memes?"

Jimmy drops his head back, exasperated. "NO! I told you, I don't even have a phone! I've never *memed* a freakin' *meme* in my life!"

The principal looks back at me. "Can I see them?"

This catches me off guard. "The... Yeah. Sure." I dig in my backpack for my phone and pull up the images. I'd asked Abby to send them to me, even though she didn't want to.

As he looks through them, Principal Kingsley's face falls. His cheeks start to turn red.

"Ah, wow. I'm so sorry, Ross. These are . . . these are awful. No wonder you came in loaded for bear. I'm just . . . Can you email these to me?" He holds my phone out.

Jimmy looks at me. "Can I see 'em? I mean, as long as I'm being blamed for 'em."

I just shrug, and he takes the phone from Kingsley. I watch Jimmy's face as he scrolls. He looks genuinely surprised.

"Jeez!" He hands the phone to me with something like shock on his face. "Those are brutal. You thought *I'd* do that?" He sounds like I accused him of kicking a puppy.

I shrug again and look away.

Kingsley crosses his big arms. "Okay. Look." He closes his eyes and rubs the bridge of his nose. Lets out a long breath. "This whole thing escalated quickly, and . . . Well, the person at fault is the one that made those things."

Jimmy almost comes out of his chair. "MALOY THREW A BOOK AT MY FRIGGIN' NECK!"

Kingsley puts out two calming hands. "I know, I know. Ross jumped to conclusions. But you didn't exactly handle the situation in a mature manner either, did you?"

Jimmy flops back in his chair, flabbergasted.

"Plus, you were chewing gum on school grounds. It pales in comparison to the fight, but it's against the rules." He sniffs. "I'm gonna have you mop Ms. Bayer's room after school. And if she can't get that gum out of her skirt, you're doing chores around here to work off the cost of her dry cleaning. Or whatever she needs."

Jimmy makes a *psshhh* sound and runs a hand through his hair.

Kingsley stands up behind his desk. "Unfortunately, this school has a zero-tolerance approach to fighting. You both know that."

I groan.

"Let's do this. I want you each to write an apology letter to Ms. Bayer. And you both get a day of detention. We'll figure out when that happens later, 'cause Ms. Jennings is out on maternity leave and detention is kind of on hold . . ." He drifts off like he's talking to himself more than to us. Then his eyes snap back up to mine.

"But if anyone asks, I'm putting you both on Triple Super Severe Probation. And I totally chewed you guys out, okay?"

Jimmy looks up at him, surprised. "So, what does Triple Super Severe mean?"

"Basically, nothing. Unless you do something else. But don't tell anyone that." He rubs his big hands over his face. "That part is partly for Ms. Bayer. She's—very understandably—upset, but I . . . That's just how I'm going to handle this. It's an unfortunate situation, and you're both victims in your own way. Kind of. Sort of."

We're all nodding, like some kind of weird football huddle.

"Okay." He goes over and opens the door. He raises his voice to an angry pitch. "Now get out of here, and don't let me see you two back in here again! You understand?"

Mrs. Hawley—the school secretary—averts her eyes as we walk out.

Jimmy and I walk back through the empty halls until we're close to the room.

"Sorry. I really thought . . ." I mutter.

He stops. "Listen. Those pictures or memes or whatever. They sucked." He pulls out his pouch of Big League Chew and stuffs nearly half the bag in his mouth. "But I still owe you the mother of all beatdowns. Someday when you least expect it."

He slams his shoulder into mine and skulks back into Bayer's classroom.

20

DAZE GONE BY

The next month or so goes by in a blur of guitar tabs, aching fingers, CDs, and some new and exciting side effects from the radiation.

My face, specifically the area between my right eye and my ear, starts to look like a honey-baked ham.

I spend a stupid amount of time looking at my eye area in the mirror. It begins as a faint pinkness, but grows into a bright, monkey-butt red. And it stings like fire, to match my dry, squinty eye. Dr. Throckton gives me some ointment—super gooey stuff—to keep on it at all times so the skin won't crack or bleed.

But crack and bleed it does—it's kind of nasty—so that eventually I start to look and feel like a scaly, oozing goo-monster. The ointment leaves oily spots on everything I own: sheets, pillows, coats, shirts, books, and folders. I keep it in my pack and use it constantly—in the slathering department, I'm giving Abby and her lip balm a run for their money.

On top of that, I notice kids keeping a little extra distance between me and them, like they think I'm contagious. In their defense, it does look like I have some sort of Gooey Creeping Crud.

A couple of times I get an "ulcer" on the white of my eye. It's technically like a super dry spot—and it feels exactly like you have a shard of glass in your eye. I'm not sure I've ever experienced pain like that. The day it flares up, it hurts like nothing I've ever felt to move my eye. So I sit in bed and stare at a spot on my comforter, trying everything I can to NOT MOVE MY EYES. Dr. Sheffler tells me to put a bunch of my nighttime eye goo in my eye and put a bandage over it. It's essentially a patch, so I get a handful of pirate comments—but at least a bandage looks kinda dramatic, unlike a stupid hat.

Still, the bandage can't keep the goo from running down my cheek throughout the day. So that's a good look.

Ross Maloy: Gooey Pirate.

One day in Mr. Brown's class, my pen ran out of ink, and I borrowed one from Jason Kelly. Then at the end of class, when I offered it back, he looked really quick back and forth between my face and the pen, and swallowed.

"I'm . . . I'm okay. You keep it."

It was only after he darted away that I looked at the pen. It was shiny from my goop. Then I noticed the shiny spots on the desk.

After that I started carrying these cleaning wipes that Linda uses all the time. I tried to do it without people noticing, but I'd wipe up any gooey spots I'd left behind me.

It was humiliating, like I'd committed some kind of crime. Like I was a burglar wiping his fingerprints.

But the shiny goop and the glowing angry red was still there on my face for all to see. I started sitting lower in my chair in class, just so I could casually prop my elbow on the desk and cover that side of my face with my hand. I got pretty good at it. Made it look natural and maybe even a little suave.

Then there are the headaches and the whole I-need-a-nap-all-the-time thing. Throckton said that shouldn't *technically* be from the radiation, but it's definitely happening. Maybe it's stress, or from straining my eyes and brain and fingers practicing guitar.

I find myself wishing time could speed up and slow down at the same time. I mean, the treatments are ticking off painfully slowly. When I check off the thirty-one-treatments-to-go date in my calendar, I feel like this thing will never be over. But at the same time, every day gone brings me one day closer to the day Abby leaves—which I never want to get here.

It kind of makes my brain hurt.

About a week after the memes, I'm waiting for Linda in the back parking lot when Sarah comes out. She's carrying her skateboard—she must keep it in her locker during the day.

My pulse speeds up.

"Hey." She pulls a pair of shoes out of her backpack and sits on the curb to swap them with the ones she'd been wearing. "How's it going?"

"Good." I've no idea how to converse naturally. "Waiting to . . . Treatment."

"Oh, right. Any new weird symptoms?"

"Not really."

She watches me for a second, then makes the shoe switch so quickly and elegantly it's like a magic trick.

She stands up. "You know, I haven't really said anything, but I think the hat looks pretty cool."

"Seriously?" She has to be joking. "I hate this thing. Makes me look like such a dork."

She shrugs and raises her eyebrows, and for a split second I think she's making fun of me. But then she smiles that easy, glowing Sarah smile, and I feel all warm and gooey inside like an idiot.

"Aight." She looks off into the distance. "See you tomorrow."

"Yeah."

She hops on her board and pushes off down the back drive. As she glides away, she looks back over her shoulder. "Don't watch! In case I fall!" She fakes for a second like she's all wobbly and about to go down. But she knows her way around a board.

And then she's gone—like some kind of freakin' unicorn.

I have more lessons with Frank, and even meet a couple of other members of Ripe Sponge. The drummer, Denny, looks like a bigger, scarier version of Jimmy—with long hair and arms full of tattoos—but he's actually super nice and even compliments me on my *Rick and Morty* T-shirt. Says he's heard a lot about me. Then he punches me on the arm and calls me Slugger—like he's heard about the fight. I'm not quite sure how to take that. He offers me some Twizzlers one day, which just seems so bizarre coming from this enormous Death-Metal-looking guy.

I show up one Wednesday night, about a week before Thanksgiving, just as a wild-eyed girl is storming out of the front door, screaming at Frank about how he needs to "grow up!" She slams the door on her car and backs out in a spray of gravel. As I come up the steps, Frank stands with his hands on his hips watching her drive away.

"So, that was Chelsea. *Was* being the operative term."

I look back at the cloud of dust settling over the street. "She seems great."

My fingertips develop some gnarly calluses, and the strings start to hurt less as the days go on. Frank seems impressed at how quickly they toughen up and nicknames me Tips of Steel.

I'm improving, and Frank gets me started on scales. I find a series of YouTube videos that are super helpful, and watch them over and over, playing along. I practice them enough that one day Linda stops by my room and asks with a pained smile and the most syrupy sweet voice ever, "So . . . when do you start playing actual songs, honey?"

My dad enjoys sitting in my room listening to my plucking. He lies back with his eyes closed and his dress-socked feet propped up on my bed. He folds his hands on his chest and smiles like my fumbling scales are the coolest jazz record ever. He barely makes a face when I hit wrong strings.

On the afternoon of Thanksgiving, I'm playing while my dad lies on the floor, listening and fighting off a food coma. To say Linda went overboard is the understatement of the year.

At some point he spots my mom's bound sketchbook on the shelf under my nightstand.

I see him grab it, and I stop playing for a second.

"Wow," he says, turning it over in his hands. "I haven't seen this in a while. Can I look inside?"

"Um . . ."

He must hear something in my voice. He sets it back where it was. "Nope. Never mind. Sounds like it's private."

"Well . . ." I start playing again. "It's not like a Dear Diary thing. Just . . . stuff . . ."

"Like mother, like son." He smiles. "Your mom kind of kept it for herself as well. I think that's cool. That's what it should be."

I play for a bit before he goes on. "You probably don't remember how much she loved Thanksgiving, do you?"

"Not really."

"She really did. It was an Event." His foot is tapping along. "And her mashed potatoes. Wowza."

"That good?"

"Songs will be written about her mashed potatoes, Ross. Stories passed down in the history books. Linda tries super hard, but . . ." He casts a quick, guilty look at the door to make sure she isn't standing there. Gives me a little shake of the head that says they're not the same.

"I don't know what she used to put in those things, but . . ."

I keep playing, and he eventually begins snoring.

Abby tolerates my practicing as well, and even quizzes me on different chords from some flash cards I made up.

She admits she has no idea if the chords I play are

correct, but she keeps throwing them at me anyway.

"Gimme an E, hotshot!"

She gets me a book with the tabs for some Vampire Weekend songs. I can't say I'm a *huge* fan—that's her thing—but thanks to Abby, those songs have been playing in the background since we were little. Like the soundtrack of our lives, as corny as that sounds.

She wants me to try and play this one song, but it has an F chord in it. It's literally the first chord in the song.

I can't play an F chord, and I'm pretty sure I'll never be able to. It's that simple. I'm fairly sure it requires ten-inch alien fingers. You have to clamp down a couple strings with your first finger and then stretch your second and third . . . Just trust me. It's the worst.

One day I walk into my lesson and set down my guitar.

"What is up with the F chord?"

Frank is in the kitchen in a Blasters T-shirt. He looks up and smiles. "Right?"

"I can't do it!"

Frank walks in and opens a Diet Coke with a loud crack. "Yeah. It's the bane of every beginning guitar player. And I swear it was in every song I wanted to play when I started."

I drop down onto the couch. "I think it's a conspiracy. To keep out people who aren't serious."

Frank drains half the can. "Maybe. It's not a bad theory."

"There isn't a trick? An easier way to get that same sound?"

He motions for me to pick up the guitar. "Practice, practice, practice."

I groan and fall over sideways, my hat tumbling to the floor. "That's your answer to EVERYTHING."

That night, we put up our Christmas tree, and I find that beat-up old red envelope, lying in the bottom of the cardboard box with a bunch of fake pine needles. As I pull it out, I try to remember what I wrote to myself.

While my dad wrestles to put the top third of the tree in its trunk, I sit down on the couch and pull out my note.

Dearest Future Ross -
Hey! How's it going? Are you
KICKING BUTT AND TAKING NAMES
this YEAR? SeventH GRADe!
LOOK AT YOU!
I BeT YOU HAVe a GIRLFRIeND,
DON'T YOU? SARAH? IS IT SARAH?
(HA. JUST KIDDING.)
Hope YOUR YeaR is Awesome.
HAVe A GOOD HOLIDAY! SAY Hi TO
ABBY AND ISAAC...
          -YOUR OLD PAL, PAST
                              ROSS

What a difference a year can make.

21

THE CLUMP

On the Tuesday morning after Thanksgiving break, I come downstairs to a frantic Linda. One of her clients got the time wrong and is waiting at a house for a showing. So we jump in the car and leave early without time to pack a lunch for me. That means cafeteria food today.

At lunch, I head to the cafeteria and get in line, overjoyed at the prospect of slimy Salisbury steak and peanut-butter-filled celery sticks. Abby said she'd try to hold a seat by the windows.

As the line inches past the bulletin board, I see a flyer there that catches my eye.

Attention:
People needed for the
Talent Show Planning Committee
If interested, talk to Sarah Kennedy

Interesting.

An opportunity to talk to Sarah. A built-in reason to *spend time* with Sarah. My wheels start spinning.

When I get to the sneeze guards, it turns out today's lunch is pizza. Granted, it's that weird square pizza with cheese that tastes kind of sweet, but pizza is pizza. The day is looking up. Even the green beans don't look too wrinkly.

Abby waves me over to a spot way back in the corner. It's by the windows that look out at a brick wall, which isn't great, but I can't really complain. We don't usually eat in here. People in the cafeteria can be pretty territorial.

I set my tray down as I spot Sarah in line with her friends—Denise Willard (we refer to her as Denise the Unpleasant) and Angie Moosebottom. (I'm not trying to be funny—that's her real last name.) Sarah is getting her food, and she's ahead of the other two. If I time this right . . .

Abby is chewing slowly, watching me. "What's up?"

Before I can think about it and psych myself out, I go. "Watch this." I give her a cheesy wink. I'm really doing this!

I cross the room quickly. Determined. Sarah grabs her milk and turns just as I step up to her.

"Hey."

She gives me an unsure smile. "Hi."

Suddenly—I mean, like, in one second flat—my heart is pounding, my mouth has gone dry, and my hat is making my head itch like crazy. Zero to basket case in 1.1 seconds.

"So, flyer. I . . . flyer." My mouth has abandoned me. Normal human grammar too. I start gesturing, hoping it'll help get my point across. "On the thing. About the thing."

Why is my head itching so bad? The spot is up under the edge of my hat. Maybe it's some kind of subconscious thing trying to distract me from my embarrassment.

Then Denise and Angie step up, in matching Taylor Swift shirts. I'd really hoped this interaction could be done before they arrived. A group is so much scarier than a single person. Plus, Denise is . . . well, she's unpleasant. I've wondered why Sarah hangs out with her.

Now they're all looking at me, and I have that panicky feeling they're really looking at my red, gooey eye. Or my dime slot.

"COMMITTEE!" I manage to blurt out. "Talent show committee! I'm interested. In helping."

"Oh!" Sarah seems relieved I'm not having some kind of mental break. Denise gives her a why-are-we-talking-to-this-person look. I seize the moment to jam my hand up under my hat to scratch.

This next part happens in slow motion.

Sarah starts to respond. "I think we have enough people, but we can always use . . ."

I finish what might be the best-feeling scratch of all time and pull my hand down.

Something comes with it.

A blur.

My heart stops as I watch it fall toward Sarah's tray. All four of us watch it, actually. It falls toward her little square of pizza.

There's a moment after the ENORMOUS CLUMP OF MY HAIR lands on the cheesy surface of Sarah's pizza before anything happens. A pause. I flash back to Dr. Throckton warning me that my hair might start falling out, but he said NOTHING about it coming out in clumps in front of the most amazing girl ever in the middle of a crowded cafeteria.

I have time to notice that some of my eye goop is mixed in with the hair, holding it together and making it look waaay grosser.

And it's a big wad. Like a little hamster perched on her slice.

My eyes fly up.

Sarah's face morphs in disgust. It's just a reflex. She recovers fairly quickly, but I see it.

Then Denise lets out a loud "EWWWWW-UH!!" Loud enough that everyone in the cafeteria stops. Like in a movie when you hear that record scratch sound, and everybody freezes. At least that's how it seems to me.

I'm not sure if this makes it better or worse, but my hand darts out and grabs the furry mess before I know I'm doing it. I shove it in my pocket.

"Oh! Oh no. I'm so sorry!"

We're all looking at it. At the pizza. A number of strands are still there, stuck to the drying grease.

Denise chimes in. "That is so nasty." She puts a hand to her chest. Like she might barf. Angie is nice enough to just step back.

"Sarah, I'm so . . ." I'm panicking. "It's from my . . ." I don't want to say, *It's okay, the doctor said this would start happening,* or the word *cancer,* or the word *treatments.*

Somehow, any of that makes it worse. More . . . contagious, even though it isn't. "I'll get you a new tray." I take it from her. She just looks kind of stunned.

I turn for the line. Every face in the room is still turned our way.

I walk up to Ms. Banfield—the lunch lady—and hand her the tray. Even she's stopped.

"Sarah needs a new tray. I . . ."

Whether she knows exactly what happened or not, she just gives me a quick nod and takes the tray.

A minute later, I walk a new lunch over to Sarah, who's sitting at her usual spot with her friends. She takes the tray from me—Denise and Angie watching—and I swear my face is burning at a million degrees.

"Ross . . ." She stops, unsure what to say.

I start to say something, but no sound comes out. So, I just smile and back up. Give her two thumbs-ups and a quick bow for some reason.

As I sit down across from Abby, she's watching me, concerned. I clutch my tray for a while, staring down at my hairless pizza.

Finally, Abby speaks. "Well, *that* could have gone better."

I shake my head. No. Not now.

22

HEAD FULL OF BEES

That afternoon I run through a cold, heavy drizzle to Linda's car. Once I'm in, I lift my hat a little and use a Kleenex to round up some of the hair that falls out. I can feel Linda watching me.

"You okay, Ross? It looks like you're starting to lose some hair there."

I stop and glare at her.

"Gee. Do you really think so, Linda?" I know it's jerky, but it feels really good to say it. Like pushing on a loose tooth with my tongue.

To her credit, Linda doesn't give up. "Hey. I get it. I'd be upset too." She gives me a sad smile. "Your hair is part of you. But just remember it's temporary. You'll be back to normal again really soon."

There's that word again. *Normal*.

Unfortunately, she caps it off with a big, loud, gurgly sip from her nearly empty Bucky's tea.

I snap.

"That's great! Thank you! I'll remember that, Linda, as me and my temporary ABNORMALNESS wallow around tonight on our HAIRY FREAKIN' SHEETS!" It's coming out, and I'm not really in control now.

"Maybe, Linda—just maybe—we can ride along in SILENCE now, so I can contemplate my IMPENDING RETURN TO NORMALCY in a few short months!" I'm bolt upright in my seat, and it takes all I have not to rear back and kick the dashboard.

Linda looks over at me with her eyebrows up and holds out a hand in surrender. "Okay. Whoa . . . I'm sorry, Ross. We're all learning as we go here, but clearly I hit a nerve. I know you're upset about Abby moving too. It's a lot to take. I'm . . . I'm really sorry, honey."

I pull my backpack into my lap and glare out the rain-streaked window.

"Linda, can you not call me honey?"

■ ■ ■

Four minutes later, I stalk into the lobby of the radiation center and brush the water out of my hair. I feel like my head is full of bees.

"Hey, hey! Dime Slot! How are we today?"

Jerry's in his usual spot, smiling and lifting his coffee at me. I don't know how to react. I feel like a raw nerve. I'm hardly in the mood to socialize. I stand still and take a few deep breaths. When I feel like I can function again, I walk over to the couches.

"Hi, Jerry."

He looks me up and down. "You look like dookie, son." He chuckles, which leads to a few phlegmy coughs.

I sit a couple of couches away. "Yeah, I'm just . . ."

Jerry nods. "That's cool. I get it." He picks up his magazine.

I flop back against the couch and close my eyes.

There's no music playing today. The only sounds are the rain and the occasional page turn from Jerry. He seems like he's into his article. I glance over at the reception desk, but nobody's manning it this afternoon. I look back as Jerry licks a big finger and turns another page.

"Seemed like a pretty good head of steam you had, comin' in here." He doesn't look up.

I feel my shoulders loosen. "Sorry."

Without moving his head, he looks over at me. "You don't need to apologize to me. "

I take off my hat and run a hand through my hair—and see a small clump fall to the carpet.

I should pick it up, but I don't. "It just . . . It's just a lot."

"Oh, sure." Jerry sets down his magazine and shifts in his seat. "I had one *doozie* of a snit last week. Over a cold bowl of broccoli cheddar soup, of all things. Marilyn still isn't real happy with me."

I nod. "My hair. It's falling out. I don't know. I mean, I have the hat—it hides it—so it shouldn't even matter."

Jerry nods. "Oh. It matters. Matters plenty. That's a tough thing." He runs a big hand over his bald head. "Lost mine a long time ago, but that was different."

I'm really tired. Like, my bones feel tired.

"What day you on, Ross?"

"I have sixteen treatments left." I look sideways at him. "But who's counting."

He gives a one-puff laugh. Nods for a while.

"This . . ." He waves a hand around at the waiting room. "All of it . . . it's a big thing, Ross. Especially at your age." Jerry grunts a bit as he gets up and heads to the coffee station for a refill. "You're supposed to be out playin' ball and chasin' the young ladies."

Now I laugh. "I'm not much of a lady chaser. At least I'm not very good at it."

"But you get what I mean." He pours half a cup and comes over to the chair closest to me. "This isn't normal, what you're doing. What *we're* doing. It's weird."

I let my head drop back and talk to the ceiling. "Jerry? Can I tell you how sick I am of being *different*? I hate it! You have no idea what I'd give to be normal. Like, a normal kid with a normal hatless head, and a goopless eye, and a normal life, and friends who aren't moving away and . . . and hair and . . ." I taper off, realizing I'm whining.

"Why?"

I tip my head and look at him like he's lost his marbles. "You're asking why I wish I *didn't have cancer*?"

Jerry scratches at some silver stubble on his cheek. "No. No, I definitely understand that part. But you talk about 'normal' a lot. What's so great about being normal?"

I stare back. "Because it's . . . normal. I don't know. Normal is normal. Why is 'good' good? Why is 'tasty' tasty? Normal's just the thing you shoot for."

Jerry scoots forward. Rubs his palms together. "See, that's where I think you're wrong." He pulls a handkerchief out of his back pocket and wipes his nose. Blows it. "I don't think normal is a goal. At least not a worthy one."

Oh no. I feel a lecture coming on. I look at the electric doors for Frank.

"What if everyone was completely normal, Ross? Have you ever thought of that? It'd be really boring, if you ask me."

I sniff and fidget.

He goes on. "But *different*! That's another matter. *Different* moves the needle. *Different* is where the good stuff happens. There's strength in different."

I scratch at my forehead and lower my eyelids at him. "So, I should be glad my cancer makes me different? I'm missing your point."

"Nah." He sits back. Waves it away with his big hand. "And I'm not sure what my point is, either. Look at me trying to be the magical old man who dispenses wisdom like he's some kinda . . . I don't know."

He shifts around in his seat. "My dad . . . he was

a hard guy. Practical. He . . . So I was pretty good at trumpet. Thought I could be a pro. Chet Baker, Louis Armstrong, all that, but he . . ." He looks uncomfortable talking about this but goes on. "'But, son, that's not what people do. Normal people.' He drilled that into me, and I . . . I stopped playing. Sold appliances 'cause that's what . . ." He stops, lost in thought. "I was good. I mean, *really* good, but he . . . I think about that all the time."

He tapers off. Shakes his head and laughs. "Sorry about that. Went off on a tangent there, didn't I? Not sure what my trumpet dreams have to do with your situation, but . . . " He smiles. "This is what happens when you get old."

I give him a weak smile. "No. I think I get what you're saying. I mean, kind of. Maybe."

He laughs. "Never mind. Eat your vegetables and stay in school. Anything else is just me talkin' outta my neck."

He picks up his magazine and crosses his legs, and I notice for the first time that he's wearing bright blue SpongeBob SquarePants socks.

I grab a Coke, go over to the window, and sip it while I stare out at the cold drizzle.

I can't believe I yelled at Linda like that.

23

UGH

After my treatment, on the way to Abby's, I apologize to Linda. She waves it off like nothing happened—"No worries!"—and takes me by Dagwood's for a cookies 'n' cream milkshake. Milkshake Therapy, she calls it. Sometimes she's pretty okay.

When I show up, Abby's parents are on their living room couch, looking at houses for sale in Minneapolis on a laptop.

We have a brief, awkward conversation about them

moving—both of them look at me with sad eyes and tell me it really is an opportunity they can't turn down—until Abby pulls at my elbow and we head for the basement. The TV is on, and Abby's been watching the old movie *Plan 9 from Outer Space*, her math homework spread out on the carpet in front of the couch.

"Is it hard?" I ask. "I haven't even looked at it yet, today was so crazy." I think about the look on Sarah's face in the cafeteria and groan.

Abby plops down on the couch and pulls her legs up, stretching her black T-shirt over them. "It's fine. You'll manage." She looks over. "There's a new meme. Do you want to see it?"

I sigh. Already? "I really don't think I do. What is it?"

"You, but bald."

"Yeah, I don't think I can . . . I don't need that today." I look at her, but her eyes are on the TV. I start to go on, but she shushes me. Gives me a look. On the TV, Vampira is walking through thick fog. We've seen this thing a dozen times. It's a cheesy old black-and-white movie, complete with super fake UFOs hanging from strings.

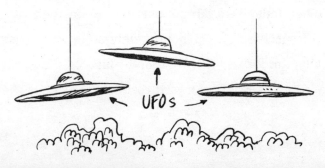

"What's with you?"

Abby pulls her eyes away, looking irritated. "What do you mean, what's with me? I'm trying to watch this." Then she's back to the movie.

We sit watching for a while in silence. At one point I go to the basement fridge, but it's pretty much empty. There's tension in the air, like electricity.

Finally, the movie ends, and Abby turns off the TV. After a few long moments, she turns and makes a face at me. "Sorry. I'm kind of freaking out." She sighs and closes her eyes. "Like a freak."

I nod for a second, and I know it's stupid and petty before it's even out of my mouth, but I say, "Oh, is your hair falling out too?"

The reaction is immediate. Abby's smile vanishes, and the temperature in the room drops.

"No, Ross." She stares. "It isn't."

"Oh. Interesting." I start picking at the sole of my Converse. "And did you humiliate yourself in front of the entire school today?"

Her stare is a glare now. "No, Ross. I didn't."

"Okay. Yeah. Well, I did."

"I know, Ross. And I'm genuinely sorry about that. I really am. But right this second—just for one teensy little moment—this isn't about you."

I haven't gotten Truly Angry Face from Abby in a while, but here it is. Her chin is starting to jut out, which means trouble.

"Maybe I need just one second of concern for me. Would that be okay? Could we maybe pencil that in?"

I look away, and she stands up. "Do you realize my whole life is about to change? Everything! I'm being uprooted! Why am I even bothering with homework? It's not like anything matters. It's so stupid. I mean, I know you're dealing with a lot—I can't imagine—but for God's sake, Ross! Am I not allowed to have my own—"

Her voice breaks as her mom's voice comes from the top of the stairs. "You booger butts need a pizza or something?"

Neither of us answers for a few seconds, so her mom tries again. "Bagel Bites?"

"We're fine, Mom." Abby goes over and drops into a chair against the wall. Tucks her legs up and wraps her arms around her knees. Starts chewing on her hair like she does. She won't look at me.

I put my head back and let out a long sigh. "Look, Abby, I'm sorry. I'm just . . ." I take off my hat, revealing my thinning area. "This day has really—"

Abby cuts me off. "No."

I look up. Abby is staring at the floor.

"Nope. Not tonight, Ross. I just can't tonight. I'm deal-ing with my own garbage. Sorry."

Wow. I slowly put my hat back on, and we sit there without speaking for a minute.

"Gotcha. Real nice." I stand up. "Selfish much?"

Abby's eyes flash fire at me. "ME? YOU'RE calling ME selfish? I bend over *backward* for you, Ross! I'm happy to do it, but WOW! You think *I'M* the selfish one? Wake up. This whole cancer thing hasn't been a cakewalk for me either, you know? I mean, Isaac . . . and other kids . . . There are . . ." Then she just runs out of words.

I turn and leave the basement without saying anything else. I feel like I might hurl. Apparently, I can't go to Abby's without storming out of the house these days.

When I get home, I go straight to my room and crawl into bed. Part of me knows I was a jerk with Abby, but another part of me is so mad I don't care.

Does she really think her problems even *compare* to mine? I mean, I have a life-threatening disease! I could friggin' *die!* And the whole Abby-is-moving problem affects me too! On *top* of all the hair falling out and people thinking I'm gross and feeling like crap and everything! So sorry you have to go to a new school with a fresh start and your cousin's super popular friends and all. I mean, boo-freakin'-hoo.

My face burns and my dry eye stings and there's hair all over my pillow and I have a throbbing headache and the simple act of rolling over feels like it would require superhuman levels of strength.

This pity party is in full swing.

Maybe I could switch schools. Surely a dumb story about hairy pizza wouldn't make its way across town. Would it?

A little later, my dad knocks and sticks his head in. "You okay in here?"

"No."

He comes in and closes the door behind him. He has a legal pad and a pen in his hand, but comes in and sits at the end of the bed. "Wanna talk about it?"

"No." I put my head back and close my eyes. "Abby and I got into it."

"Mmm." I feel the bed shake a little as he nods his head. "Sorry. But you guys'll work it out, I'm sure."

He sits there long enough that I finally open an eye to make sure he's okay. He's just looking around at my stuff. My Star Wars Lego sets. I close my eyes again.

"Aren't I—y'know, since I have cancer—aren't I supposed to have some big epiphany?"

He sets his pad and pen down. "How do you mean?"

"I mean, on TV, I see people on the *Today Show*. Shows like that. Talking about how being sick taught them that every day is"—I make quote marks with my fingers—"'a precious, wonderful gift from above.' That I should cherish every day and live every moment like it's my last."

I look at him when he doesn't answer right away.

"Yeah. I've heard those people. You're not feeling that?"

I sit up against the headboard and cross my arms. "No. No. I'd say I'm much more in the 'every day is an endless slog of misery' camp right now."

My dad chuckles and runs a hand over his face. "Ah-hhhhh." One more laugh. "I think that's probably okay, Ross. I'd guess that's fairly normal. It's just not gonna get you on the *Today Show*."

I sit staring off for a minute. "I mean, I don't get an epiphany?"

He smiles. "Well. Not yet, I guess. Maybe it's coming. Bubbling up from way down in your toes."

I knock my head against the headboard a couple times, lightly. "Great."

He sits there a while longer, waiting to see if there's more. Eventually he grabs his pad and thumps it against my leg. "Okay. I have a ton of stuff I've gotta work through. Don't be too hard on yourself, okay?"

I nod.

He gets up. Turns as he's about to leave the room. "Any word from Isaac?"

I just look at him and give him the smallest perceptible shake of my head.

He nods a bit. "That's disappointing." Then he closes the door softly behind him.

I vaguely remember slogging down the stairs to eat a fourth of my dinner at some point. (Tuna and noodles, yay.) Then it's back to my room for more ceiling staring.

The next morning, it's not hard to convince my dad and Linda that I don't feel up for school—I barely need to move my lips to tell them. All energy and will to live has fled the building.

They're both concerned, but my dad is in charge of two big meetings about the insurance case that he can't miss. Linda says she can move some things around and work from home, and I hear her puttering around downstairs throughout the day. She drops in with snacks a few times, but I'm not hungry.

"Hey, Ross. I know you're miserable right now, but it'll get better, okay?"

I grunt into my pillow as she comes in and rubs my back. She sits on the edge of the bed for a bit. Smooths my hair in the back. Eventually I fake some deep breaths like I'm falling asleep, and she quietly leaves. When I finally roll over, I find two fun-sized Butterfingers—my favorite—next to the pillow. I eat them, joylessly, but appreciate the gesture.

I stay in bed. At one point I pull out my mom's leather sketchbook and draw a little imaginary landscape like she used to do. I grab one of her other old sketch journals and flip through some of her drawings and wonder if they were some of the last ones she did. What was she feeling when she did them? There's one really beautiful one of a creek and some trees, with pencil lines so light they look like they could float away. Like she did.

I may not remember her as well as my dad does, but I miss her in my bones.

At one point I lay the guitar beside me and lightly brush its strings, but for the most part, I just lie there until that afternoon, when I have no choice.

It's time for another treatment.

24

MORE GREAT NEWS

The waiting room is empty. I'm slumped over sideways, zoned out on a couch, when Frank comes into the lobby.

"Hey. You ready?"

I notice his lack of Frankness right away. I wonder if this depression thing is going around. Like the flu. Heaving myself out of bed felt like lifting a two-thousand-pound bag of wet sand.

"Yeah." I push myself up and follow him through the doors. Even Frank's walk is slower than normal, so I have to ask. "What's up?"

Frank looks over. "Ah, we just found out Jerry's in the ER. Got sick really fast last night. He had a really bad night and morning. Sounds like it's pneumonia." He holds the door to the treatment room for me. "Marilyn

—his wife—called to let us know he wouldn't be in."

I'm alarmed. Maybe even stunned a little. "But I talked with him yesterday. He seemed fine. I mean, he was coughing a lot, but he always does."

Callie, sitting at the controls, spins around in her chair and gives me a smile as she gets up. "I'm sure he'll be okay. We just like the old guy, you know? And pneumonia at his age isn't . . ."

We all stand awkwardly, with our hands on our hips. Then Frank shakes it off.

"He'll be fine. I've told that guy twenty times that if he dies, I'll kill him." He leans in for a closer look at the red, flaky skin around my eye. "Yeesh. Are you keeping the goo on there? It's looking angry."

I stick my jacket and cowboy hat in the locker in slow motion. "Trust me. I eat, sleep, and breathe goo."

Minutes later, I'm lying on the gurney wondering if this day could get worse when Callie steps up. She leans over me as she locks my mask into place. "You okay?"

I take a second to answer her. "That . . . is a really complicated question."

She laughs. "Yeah. You're in the thick of this now. I noticed you're losing hair." She leans in for a closer look. "The eyebrow's starting to go too."

If my head wasn't locked down, I'd sit up.

"It is?"

Callie nods. "Yeah . . . it is. Sorry. It's thinning. But the hair'll grow back pretty quickly."

I feel like I need to get up. If only to find a mirror. "The hair will, but not the eyebrow. I heard that's permanent."

Frank steps up. "Having two eyebrows is waaaaay overrated. You wanna be just like everybody else?"

"Yes!" I nod as much as the mask will let me. "Yeah, I very much do!"

Callie pushes a few buttons on the panel beside her. "Well, too late, buddy! You're special!"

I close my eyes and groan. "Well, being special sucks."

Frank smiles and points at the equipment. "All right, Tips of Steel. You know the drill."

My dad drops me off for my guitar lesson a few minutes before six thirty.

"I'm going to AT&T." His antique of a phone has finally given up the ghost. "I'll be back in an hour unless it takes longer than that. If so, just . . . wait. I'll be here." He pats me on the back before I get out.

As I come through the screen door, Frank is still in his scrubs from work, messing with an electric guitar on the dining room table.

"Is that new?"

He looks up. "Old, actually. And ruined. It's a long story, but Denny backed over it last weekend after our show. It's toast."

He picks it up as I walk over.

"See there?" The body is cracked, and the surface has deep scrape marks. "If I only teach you one thing in this life, let it be this: Never let the drummer drive."

I nod. "Got it."

He walks over to the couch and pushes a bunch of wrinkled copies of *Guitar Player* magazine onto the floor.

"Also, never trust a guy in pleated pants. That's not related. It's just good life advice." He plops down and crosses his feet on the coffee table.

I hear a crash from the back of the house. "Who's that?

Frank looks in that direction. "Denny. He's in his room studying for some entrance exam. Wants to repair fridges, which pays better than being in a failing band. And they don't care if you have tattoos of Willie Nelson and Elvis Presley down your arms."

He starts clapping his hands.

"Let's go! Play me some beautiful scales, Coin Slot!"

I pop open the guitar case. "It's Dime Slot." Then I lift out the guitar, grab a pick, take a deep breath—and proceed to play a painful series of wrong notes, mistakes, and screwups. My fingers have a mind of their own. Frank stops me.

"Okay. Wow. That was god-awful." He nods like he's thinking it over. "I don't even know what you were trying to do there. Just . . . relax. Breathe. And try again."

I take another deep breath and start again . . . with even worse results.

Frank has one eyebrow raised. "You in there today? You okay?"

"Yeah, I'm okay." I have to sniff after I say it. I'm not okay. My good eye is blurring with water, and the bad one is stinging like acid. I look up and lean back, trying to stop it from going any further.

"I'm just . . . Gah! Give me a second."

Frank nods slowly, watching, while I fish out some eye drops. He grabs a Kleenex from the box on the side table and hands it to me.

I let out a long breath. I've been numb all day, just staring at the ceiling. Now it's like the guitar playing has pushed the On button for all my emotions. Maybe if

I stay still enough, my thoughts'll calm down and stop pinging off the inside of my skull like a pinball machine.

Frank picks up his own guitar and starts playing it quietly. Effortlessly.

"This isn't about Jerry, is it?"

"No." I close my eyes. "I mean, yes. That . . . and other stuff. A bunch of stuff."

He picks through a couple of chord progressions. "Such as?"

"Well. There's just a lot . . ." I lift my head. Stare at a dent in the side of the trunk table. Rub my eyes with the back of my hand.

"Spill, buddy. I don't have anywhere to be."

So I do.

"My best friend and I aren't speaking . . . and she's moving in a few weeks . . . I was a total jerk to my stepmom . . . My hair's falling out, and my eyebrow's gone for good . . . And my other friend, Isaac, has just vanished . . . acts like he barely knows me . . . My face and eye hurt . . . I managed to embarrass myself in front of this awesome girl, and my entire . . ." It just keeps coming. Like word barf. Once I start, the floodgates open.

I tell him everything that's happened plus a good amount of the garbage swirling around in my head. As I ramble like a lunatic for five or ten minutes, barely taking a breath, Frank slowly stops picking out notes.

He just nods, making quick comments like "Whoa" and "Aw, man."

After my rant, the room feels extra quiet.

I take a couple of deep breaths and scratch up under my hat—carefully. We sit in silence for almost a minute.

"That's tough stuff, Ross." He's looking down at his guitar. "I'd say your plate is . . . full. Too full, by far. And those memes, that's just . . ." He tapers off.

"Yeah." I'm back to staring at the trunk.

He plucks a couple of notes. "I'm searching my brain for something smart to say. Some piece of advice that'll make things better, but all I can think of is 'Screw 'em.'"

I let out a puff of a laugh.

He goes on. "Sometimes life is just the WORST, y'know? Sometimes it can be hard as hell. All you can do is ride it out, and maybe . . . focus on the things you love? The people you love? And just kind of . . . hang on. With both hands."

He sighs, and we sit there for a few seconds in silence.

Finally, Frank looks up at me. "Do you like blowing stuff up?"

"I . . ." I'm not sure I heard him right. "Like, with explosives?"

Frank sets his guitar down. "No. Like video games. Denny's got some new game—it just came out. *Mars* something."

"Wait. Not *Annihilation: Mars*?"

Frank snaps. "That's it."

I scoot forward on the couch. "That doesn't come out for a month."

Frank shrugs. "Yeah, I don't know about this stuff. But Denny knows a guy who tests games or something? Got him a bootleg copy. I bet he'd let us play."

I look down at the guitar in my lap. "Now? And not finish the . . ."

Frank gives me a look. "You're not in your head. Nothing's gonna stick today, and I don't blame you. I think blowing stuff up on a foreign planet would be a lot more productive."

Then he yells at the top of his lungs, "DENNY! STUDY BREAK!"

Ten minutes later, Denny and Frank are cheering as I storm an alien compound, plasma guns blazing. Best of all, the TV is about three times louder than anything my dad and Linda will put up with when Frank shouts, "Turn it up more!"

Denny grabs the remote and puts it up even further, until the windows are shaking. For a guy who doesn't like technology, Frank has a pretty amazing surround sound system.

With Frank and his giant tattooed drummer looking on, I kick in the compound's front portal and lay gory, violent waste to mountains of hostile bug-faced alien freaks, a fine mist of blood and entrails in my wake.

And it feels *gooood*.

When Denny can't take it anymore, he grabs the controller from me and takes a turn. He's pretty funny to watch, ducking and leaning around on the couch yelling, "Oooh! Don't eat me, you crazy-faced alien $%#@&!"

Denny's character is digging through the rubble for health and energy packs when he leans over and bumps my shoulder with his.

"You know, Jimmy's pretty decent on drums. You guys should get together and jam sometime."

My stomach drops.

"Oh. That's . . . that's okay. I'm good."

Denny jumps when an alien pops out from a storage closet—blasts it—and laughs.

"No, seriously. I know you aren't exactly best friends, but who cares?"

Frank is pointing at the screen. "There. Behind the control thingy. One of the green packs." Denny collects it.

I walk over to the sink and pour water into a faded IU cup. "'Not best friends' is putting it pretty lightly. He said he still owes me a beatdown."

Denny makes a dismissive sound. "Whatever. He's all bark. I'll set him straight if he—GYYAAAAHHHH!!"

Onscreen, his character's head is being eaten by a red monkey-looking thing. He falls back into the couch. Flings the remote to Frank and looks over.

"I'll talk to him."

"It's . . ." This whole thing is making me squirm. "Don't bother. If there's one thing I can tell you, Jimmy and me playing together is never going to happen."

25

JIMMY

My dad's dropping me off at Frank's just as Jimmy pulls onto the gravel driveway on a beat-up old ten-speed. It's way too small for him, making him look a little like a grizzly on a tricycle.

He doesn't acknowledge us.

After locking up his bike, he climbs the front steps right behind me, and nudges me out of the way. I stand back as he opens the door. He lets the screen door slap shut in my face.

I shake it off.

I knew things were off when Jimmy sat down beside me in class this morning. I could feel him staring at me, so I looked over. He huffed and looked away, chewing loudly. So, I bent to get my books out and could tell he was looking over again.

I jerked my head up. "What?"

"*What?*" He shot me an angry look and rolled his eyes away to the front of the room, shaking his head like he couldn't believe this was happening. Closed his eyes and let out a huge sigh.

"So, my cousin . . ." He mumbled it and tapered off, scratching at his hat-squished hair.

"Denny."

He sat up and looked at me like I was an idiot. "Yeah. Denny. My cousin." It looked like this conversation was killing him.

"Yeah." I nod. "He told me you play drums. That you're pretty good."

He glared at me a bit more, then waved his hand. "He says we should go over tonight and try playing. Or whatever."

I made a quick mental note to kill Denny.

I stared at the top of my desk for a bit. Sarah came in and sat down in front of me, and I thought once again about how she always smells like sunshine and joy. A vision flashed through my head of her watching me play at the talent show.

I turned to Jimmy. "I'm okay with that if you are."

Jimmy nodded a couple of times. "Whatever. Fine. Only 'cause Denny has himself all in a twist about it."

Now we're both here. Frank and Denny take us down to the basement. It's unfinished, and they've covered the walls with blankets and tapestries to muffle the sound. There's a big backdrop hanging between the high windows with *RiPE SPoNgE* in swirly letters. Half a dozen amplifiers are scattered around. Electric guitars on stands. A keyboard. A drum set.

"Welcome to the lair, Ross." Frank picks up an acoustic guitar and starts checking the tuning. Denny adjusts the height of a cymbal.

Jimmy goes over and throws a leg over the stool to sit down at the drum kit. He takes a pair of sticks out of his back pocket and tests the sound of a few drums.

Jimmy and I still haven't spoken to each other since we got here.

Frank plugs a cord into the end of the guitar. An electric acoustic? I have to admit I didn't even realize that was a thing. I take it and put the strap over my head, noticing the hum of the amp.

I look up, and Denny and Frank are looking at me. Then Denny jumps like he forgot something. "Wait! Wait! We need rock-and-roll lighting." He flips on a couple of lamps and shuts off the overhead lights. "Need the right look. This could be a historic moment. Like Keith Richards and Mick Jagger in a studio for the first time together."

I've read up on my Rolling Stones because of the mix. "Except Jagger didn't play drums."

Jimmy makes a disgusted sound. "And Keith Richards wasn't a little zit-faced dork!" He shoots me a death glare and points a stick at me.

"All right. Let's see what you got, Maloy!"

26

CREATIVE DIFFERENCES

Jimmy smacks his sticks together four times and then he's playing—louder and a lot faster than I expected. I look over at Frank.

Frank leans back against the windowsill, smiling. "Play something. A chord progression or . . . Just jump in!"

I watch Jimmy for a few bars—he's better than I expected—and then I go for it.

I play the simplest progression I know—the first one Frank showed me—but even so I can't change my chords fast enough. It sounds like garbage.

I fumble, then stop, and then Jimmy stops.

"What was *that*?" He looks like I wiped a booger on him. I feel my cheeks go red. I curse the fingers of my left hand.

Denny throws some kind of rag at Jimmy's head. "Slow it down, dummy! You've been playing for a year. Ross just started a few weeks ago."

Jimmy rolls his eyes and turns some knob on one of the drums. "Fine."

He thinks about it for a second, then starts in—a different beat than before. A little slower.

I wait a few bars, and then I'm in.

The first time through, the chords are kind of sloppy. But then I click into the beat. And it feels great. Like two cogs in my brain have finally synced up.

Frank is bobbing his head. Rubbing his beard. "Okay! Okay, there we go! Nice! Just keep that going a bit. Get used to it."

Jimmy's scowl fades, and a big grin spreads across my face before I even realize it.

I can't help it. This is AWESOME!

A few more times through, and I change up the way I'm strumming—a different pattern. Jimmy hears it and changes his rhythm to match it. Denny claps his enormous hands a few times and sits back on a stool. Laughs. "There ya go! A little call and response. This is MUSIC, ladies and gentlemen!" He starts bobbing his head so happily I can kind of see the nerdy band kid hiding under all the hair and tattoos.

We keep playing. After a while one of us changes something, then the other will follow and do something new. Back and forth. In a way it's like a dance.

A dance with a big goof who wants to knock my block off.

Jimmy stops and grabs a towel from beside the drum kit to wipe his forehead. He's always kind of a sweaty guy to start with, but now he's really working. Through his wad of gum, he asks Frank to hand him a cup sitting in the corner.

Denny gives us a slow clap. "That was cool. That was very cool. More fun than practicing by yourself, am I right?"

Jimmy is nodding and slyly spitting into the cup between his legs when Denny realizes what he's doing.

"Jimmy! What'd I tell you about that?" He walks over and holds an enormous hand out, waiting. "Hand it over."

Jimmy rolls his eyes, busted. Holds out the cup.

"Whatever."

Frank jumps up and takes the cup away from Jimmy.

"You can *whatever* all you want, but you're not spitting in my favorite collectible *Adventure Time* cup."

Denny keeps after him. "What have I told you about the spitting thing? It's disgusting, dude. You aren't still carrying that nasty jar around, are you?"

Jimmy looks away, embarrassed. "No."

I can't help it. I laugh. That kind of laugh that pops out of your throat like a seal bark.

"BAH!"

They all turn to look at me, especially Jimmy, and I can literally feel the heat in his glare.

Denny's eyebrows go up. "He does? He still does it?"

I look over at Jimmy—he's boring holes in me with his eyes—then back at Denny.

"I dunno. Maybe?" Denny puts his hands on his hips like that isn't good enough. "Yeah. A lot."

Denny looks really irritated as he walks over and swats Jimmy on the back of the head. "Such a bonehead! You look like a freakin' idiot. And it's DISGUSTING! Chew a normal human-sized amount if you—"

He stops when Jimmy whips a drumstick at my head. Then Jimmy's up and moving, coming around the kit. His shoulder knocks into that up-and-down cymbal thingy, and it goes down with a crash.

Then Frank is jumping between us. "Hey! Hey!" He puts his hands on Jimmy's chest, holding him back. "Guitars! Expensive gear! Chill out!"

"Little rat!" Jimmy's face is red, and he's leaning into Frank's hands. He spits his gum at me, but I step away.

"You couldn't just shut up, could you? Moron. Way to stick up for your bandmate, you—"

His words are cut off as Denny steps behind him and gets him in a headlock. Jimmy fights against the huge arm for a second before giving up.

Frank steps back beside me. "So, okay. Maybe that's good for today. But it's a jumping off point."

Denny smiles. "Yeah, I think this went really well. Same time tomorrow?"

Later, I'll admit that I hurry to my dad's car—just in case Jimmy's waiting to get in a late sucker punch. I'm home and halfway up the stairs before I remember.

Wait.

Did Jimmy refer to himself as my bandmate?

27

TAKE TWO

I look for Abby the next day—our fight has gone on too long, and I need my best friend—but I don't see her around her locker. I go to the loading dock at lunch, but she isn't there. She must be out for the day. It's freezing, but I sit on the steps eating while I text her.

Hey. Where are you? We
need to talk.

Sick.

Okay. But soon?

It's a while before her response comes through.

K.

In class, Jimmy and I ignore each other completely until the bell rings. Then he stands up and knocks my book off my desk. I look up at him, unsure what to do, and he's giving me a challenging look.

"We gonna play tonight?"

I sit looking at his big Jimmy face for a second. "Yeah. I'll be there."

He nods once and skulks out.

Jerry isn't there for his treatment again, and Frank and Callie haven't heard anything new.

Frank has yet another new mix, and we figure out that I'm a fan of the Pixies, the National, Parquet Courts, and the Ramones—a punk band from the '70s and '80s, he tells me.

"You never cease to surprise me, young Ross."

I throw my backpack over my shoulder as I head out. "You and me, both. See you in an hour."

Jimmy and I barely speak that night, but we play a *lot*. Mostly just jamming, but Frank leads us into trying a couple of songs too. A relatively simple Neil Young song. An Eagles song, even though Denny turns his nose up at the idea. It all feels really good.

Sounds halfway decent too. Kinda almost.

At one point, Denny gets a call from his now ex-girlfriend and heads upstairs to take it. Frank stands up too.

"All right. This is risky, but I have to take a leak. Can I go upstairs without you two murdering each other?"

We both nod, but it gets super weird the second Frank leaves. That kind of awkward where you keep sniffing and looking around at the corners of the room.

Then Jimmy says, "What happened with you and your girlfriend?"

I look up. "Girlfriend?"

"The weird one. Abby. With the clothes and the hair."

I swallow a burst of anger. In his defense, she *does* dress weird. "She's not my girlfriend."

Jimmy looks genuinely surprised. "Seriously? You guys're always together."

I shake my head. "Just friends."

Jimmy taps a cymbal a few times, lightly. "I figured she caught you checkin' out Sarah Kennedy."

My head jerks up.

"What?"

Jimmy laughs like I'm an idiot. "Well, you go gooey every time Sarah comes in a room."

I straighten my back, defiant. "I do not."

"Riiiiiight." He tightens a couple of turny things

on his kit. "I don't get it, but it's really obvious."

I feel my face getting red. "What don't you get?"

"The big deal about Sarah Kennedy. She's . . . super fake. She's only nice to the 'right people.' Trust me, I know."

"Really? How?"

Jimmy taps the snare drum a couple of times. "Her locker is right next to me. She and her stupid friends hang out there." He uses his pedal to hit the bass drum. "They don't hold back in front of me. I might as well be a lump of mud, as far as they care. So I hear all kindsa stuff."

I stare at him. "Yeah, well, I didn't ask you. And how are *you* gonna judge people on niceness? You, of all people."

He snort-laughs as we hear Frank's feet coming down the stairs. "I'm nice enough." He puts a hand on his chest and looks exaggeratedly sincere. "I'm just misunderstood."

Frank comes into the room with a CD player like my dad's. He picks up a bright blue electric guitar that looks a lot like the one Denny drove over with his van, but this one isn't broken. He holds it out to me.

"You guys ready to rock?" Then he looks over at Jimmy. "Jimmy? Have you ever listened to the Ramones?"

■ ■ ■

Thirty minutes later, my fingers are screaming in pain and Jimmy is wiping sweat off the back of his neck. I've never felt better in my life.

We'd listened to a song several times while Frank wrote out the chords for me—only three! Perfect! Then we got started. We crashed and burned a few times, but eventually we found our groove. And Holy Batpig, was it fun.

It felt loud and dangerous and gritty and totally 100 percent right, all at the same time. At one point, Jimmy and I both started laughing—just at the sheer volume of it—as Denny cranked my amp up to ten and told Jimmy to play harder.

I should be clear: We sounded pretty terrible. It was loose and sloppy, and we kept screwing up, but none of that mattered. We just kept going.

It felt . . . sort of like going outside and screaming at the top of my lungs—but in the best way possible. At one point I started singing part of the chorus. I wasn't even embarrassed. It just felt like . . . letting go. Frank turned a microphone on and stuck it in my face, and I just yelled the words I remembered. I made some up too.

"Rabbit! Rabbit! YO, Artichoke RAAAAAH!!!"

We've been on break for a couple of minutes, with Jimmy trying to catch his breath, when he looks over and gives me a nod. "Let's do it again."

He doesn't have to ask twice.

We run through it four or five more times, and Frank and Denny kick back watching—big stupid grins on their faces.

We finish and sloppily come to a stop as Frank gets up. He walks between Jimmy and me and holds up his hands. Starts talking in a big, loud preacher voice.

"Gentlemen! I want it on the record that glorious sounds were made here tonight. We have cast aside our demons and been filled with the spirit of the beat! Rock and roll was in! The! Room! I want you both to stand, face each other, and shake hands to acknowledge the power of this thing called music."

I go over as Jimmy gets up and leans over his drums. I shake his big sweaty hand. My body is still buzzing from the music as Jimmy laughs, out of breath.

"That was %#@$* awesome."

Later, as we're leaving, Denny pats me on the back. "Dude, that was so much fun to watch. You guys officially rocked it." I smile, and he goes on. "And listen. I know you were just kinda playing around in there . . . but you can sing."

That stops me. "Me?"

Denny's eyebrows go up. "Yeah! No joke! You guys don't need to find a singer. You can do it."

My throat goes dry at the thought of singing on stage, but I'd be lying if part of me didn't get kind of excited at the idea. I think about it while I put in some eye drops. "Huh."

"Now we just gotta find you a bass player, and you guys'll be set."

"Yeah." I stop, looking out into the nighttime neighborhood. "A bass player."

I had one person in mind. She's a pretty good musician too.

It's funny how everything always comes back to Abby.

28

BACK TO THE PAST

Getting back to my Summer Medical Follies, after seeing Dr. Throckton, we canceled one (awful) surgery and got the new one scheduled almost immediately. Like, two days later—which is nothing, and it flew by. My head was in serious danger of spinning off my head as we got ready, this was all happening so fast.

My dad and Linda invited Abby and her parents over the night before for Linda's rosemary chicken lasagna—one of my favorites. I had to stop eating at ten p.m. so my stomach would be empty enough for the surgery, so they were giving me a treat.

It was kind of an awkward dinner, and all the adults asked me how I was doing about seventy times. I don't think they even knew they were doing it.

After Mrs. Peterson's cherry pie with ice cream, Abby and I sat out on the back porch. It was perfect out, and we propped our feet up on the railing, watching a handful of fireflies doing their thing.

"Ross. I have a serious question to ask. Can I make fun of you and draw on you and stuff when you're all groggy on painkillers?" Abby was wearing green leggings and a pink Vampire Weekend tour shirt. She was playing the album *Modern Vampires of the City* quietly on her phone.

"If you must. It's not like I'll remember it." I felt like my stomach was gonna pop like a zit. I ate waaay too much.

We were quiet for a minute, listening to Vampire Weekend and a bunch of surprisingly loud crickets.

"Are you nervous?"

"A little. Not exactly. Not like you'd think." I tipped my chair back on its back legs, no parents here to tell me not to. "I'm just not thinking too much about what they'll do tomorrow. I don't really wanna know."

"Yeah. I guess the scarier thing would be NOT having the surgery at this point."

I nodded. Rocked back and forth. "Yep. I just want the bad stuff out of me."

Abby reached over and flicked my ear. "I'll be there all day tomorrow. My dad has a thing, but my mom said she'll stay with me in the waiting room."

"Eeesh. Boring. Make sure you take your phone charger. And headphones. I've got some new games I can recommend."

Abby tipped back as well. "Yeah, I'll bring a book. Some people read, Ross."

"M'kay. You have fun with that."

"Yeah." Abby's tone shifted. "Just so you know, I don't like this, Ross. Not at all. But, it's gonna go fine. Seriously. Like, no question. Okay?"

I nodded. Then we sat there, quiet. The moment stretched out for a while, all serious and heavy and kind of uncomfortable.

I said the only thing I could think of.

"Did you fart?" I knew she hadn't, but it got a laugh out of her.

The surgery was crazy early. It was pitch-black out as I put on my clothes. I wore loose shorts and a loose T-shirt like they said to, so they could get me back in them easily when I was all goofy and floppy from the drugs. Plus, it was the end of July and hotter than Hades—my dad's words—even at six a.m.

I was somehow really tired and wide awake at the same time.

A nurse in bright blue Crocs came in and wrote with a marker above each of my eyes. YES above the right and NO above the left. She showed me in a little handheld mirror.

"This is so no one makes a mistake. We don't like mistakes here."

I wasn't sure if that made me feel better or worse.

They got me all set up in a hospital bed and stuck an IV in the crook of my arm. It didn't hurt too bad going in, but the tape holding it in place kept pulling at my skin and pinching me. Then my dad and Linda and I sat there for half an hour making awkward small talk.

"How are those shorts? Comfy?" Linda had cut the legs off of some Avengers pajama pants to make them.

"Yep. Real comfy."

Eventually, after we'd talked about pajamas and the Avengers as much as I could take, the nurses came and rolled me down the hall to a surgery room—Linda waving with one hand over her mouth, my dad with watery eyes, giving me two thumbs-ups.

Then I was in the surgery room, and it was full of people and equipment. Something was beeping behind me. The anesthesiologist talked to me all softly and gently and then put some fluid in my IV line and told me to count backward from one hundred.

I got to ninety-six.

I don't remember much for a while. Out of the next ten days or so, I only remember moments, and even those are hazy.

• Getting up to pee in the hospital bathroom in the middle of the night, and blood pouring into the toilet from the bandage above my eye.

• Being wheeled out of the hospital, gorked out of my mind. Feeling my head bob around. A couple of long strings were taped from my forehead to my cheek— maybe to hold my eyelid closed?

• Linda and my dad helping me into bed. Abby helping me get my earbuds in and putting on some quiet music. (Guess which band.)

• The ceiling. Lots of staring at the ceiling. Finding faces in the texture there.

• An arrangement someone dropped off with heart-shaped cookies on sticks in a little basket. Abby unable to stop eating them.

• Linda kissing me on the forehead and asking if I needed anything about twenty times a day.

• My dad and Abby running to Dagwood's and then cutting my sub up into little manageable bits I could eat lying down. My dad singing the Dagwood's jingle as they delivered it to me.

• Feeling around with my hands—afraid to move my head—trying to find the remote to the TV my dad had brought into my room. Wanting the remote because there was a soap opera on it. Not finding it and half dreaming about the overly dramatic soap problems of Stefano and Marlena.

• My dad lying on the bed beside me watching the St. Louis Cardinals (his team forever, since he's from there), trying to cheer and react without jostling the bed. Whispering, "Sorry! Sorry!" after a three-run homer.

· Raging, splitting headaches and pain around my eye when the pills would start to wear off. Aching from lying there all day.

• Abby in a chair by my bed. Watching TV. Reading. Talking to me when I felt up to it. Abby bringing me ice packs. Abby reading me a bunch of *Bob's Burgers* comics she brought. Abby reading me articles out of her dad's old copies of *Famous Monsters* magazine.

Always Abby.

29

HAT IN HAND

Back in the Abby-and-I-still-aren't-speaking present, I have my dad drop me at her house after Jimmy's and my practice. It's a little late for a drop-by, but I need to talk to her. I can't believe we've gone this long without having a real talk, and I feel like a world-class tool.

Her mom answers the door and gives me a sad smile.

"Hi, Ross. It's really good to see you." Then she yells over her shoulder, "Abby! Visitor!"

Abby appears at the end of the hall. If she's surprised to see me, she doesn't show it. She just nods, tips her head for me to follow her. In her room, she drops into her chair.

I stop inside the door. "Abby. I'm sorry. I was a jerk. And I've continued to be a jerk."

She nods. "Yeah, you were. You have been." She sets down her glass of water. "But I was too."

"Can we just erase the past week? Let bygones be bygones and all that?"

She looks at me for a minute, then puts a hand up in the air, and relief floods my body. I go over and high-five it.

I drop my backpack and sit down on the floor, my back against her bed. "I think I've been way up my own butt."

She laughs. "Me too. I've kind of set up camp in there lately."

I laugh at the image that pops into my head.

She goes on. "I guess, you know, we both have a right to be a little selfish right now. It's just . . . a lot."

"It is a lot." I grab a little Godzilla figure from her bedside table. "How are you doing with the move?"

She shrugs. Sighs. "I've just been thinking about next semester a lot. It's gonna be hard. I'm not great at making friends."

This surprises me. "You're friends with me. And Isaac. I think."

At Isaac's name, she rolls her eyes and wobbles her head around like she isn't so sure of that.

"Yeah. I know. It'll happen. It's just gonna be weird. I kind of tend to stick out in a way not everyone is drawn to." She uses her monster-gloved hand to gesture at her neon-green Frankenstein shirt and her pink-and-orange tights.

"Abby, you don't stick out. You stand out. It's different."

She smiles at that. "Says the guy voted Most Likely to Have a Mental Breakdown if He Ever Stood Out."

I shake my head. "Ah. No, see, I don't think so. I think I'd be okay with *standing* out. Standing out, good. Sticking out, bad. In my mind, at least."

She makes an impressed face. "Interesting. The boy evolves. Is this New and Improved Guitar God Ross talking?"

"Maybe." I set Godzilla down on the carpet and think for a minute. "It's weird. I think I always just assume you're okay. You're my rock. The tough one. I guess I just figured you'd have zero problem walking into a new school and Abby-ing it up."

Abby shakes her head. "Nope. Wigging out over here." She picks some lint off of her tights. "Kind of a mess."

"Yeah. And I let you down. I've been really slow at realizing that. You're always there when I need you . . . and then I blow it."

She waves it away like a fly, and we sit quietly for a moment.

She looks up. "Can we just make a . . . y'know, a vow or a pact . . . to spend as much time hanging out as we can till I leave? Like, make the most of it?"

I smile and nod for a while. "Yeah. Absolutely. Can I help you pack?"

She looks around the room. "Definitely. Just, not tonight. I'm toast."

And I feel like this is the moment.

"Sooooo . . ." I'm unsure how to approach this. "You should know . . . I've been playing with Jimmy."

She stares back for an uncomfortably long time. "Playing what? Dolls?"

"Music, dummy. He plays drums, believe it or not. And he's actually pretty good."

She's not buying it at first, but I tell her all about it.

About our practices. The songs we've learned. How good it felt tonight.

"Wow." She looks unsure how to react. Says it again. "Wow."

"I know. It's weird. If we don't kill each other, we might . . . y'know. Talent show. World tour. Rock stardom."

She makes a face. "But . . . it's Jimmy. Yuck." Her eyes dart around as she thinks. "Maybe you can work on his hygiene. He always smells like cold french fries." She looks ill. "And the jar thing."

"We'll see. But, you know . . . baby steps. And I think he's stopped the spit thing."

I look over at her viola propped up in the corner.

"So . . . how's band? How's the cello playing?"

She lowers her eyelids at me. "It's a viola, and you know it."

I smile. I do know.

"Band is going fine. As per usual. Why?"

I look over at her sideways.

"Have you ever thought about playing bass guitar?"

30

THE PITCH

"**C**ome again?" Abby stares at me.

"Abby. Think how cool it'd—"

"Ross, I'm moving away in two weeks. *Two*. And the talent show is only two weeks away." Her eyes are all big, and she's looking at me like I'm an idiot. Her mouth is even hanging open a little bit. "You want me to learn how to play bass in that time?"

"Yes."

I sit, waiting.

She's still staring, but her eyes start flicking back and forth across the carpet. I watch her until she sits back. Closes her mouth.

"How many songs are we talking about?"

I grin. "Two or three, tops. We'll only play one, but— y'know—it's good to have options."

She turns and stares at a *Mothra* poster for maybe thirty seconds.

"I . . . This is stupid. We don't have a bass guitar in concert band. I've never even held one."

I lean in. "Frank has a bass guitar you can borrow."

She stares at me for a bit, but I can tell her mind is working overtime. I try to help. "They aren't complicated songs. You just . . . boom boom boom boom boom." I mimic her plucking one note on a bass.

Slowly, a smile spreads across her face. She shakes her head. "This is crazy."

I clap my hands. "It's AWESOME is what it is." I get up. "Think about it. Down the road, we'll go to college together and form a band. Abby and the Rosstones or something. This is just a head start."

She stands up and runs a hand through her hair. "Ross! We're seriously gonna play music together? This is so cool!" She gives me a hug, but then breaks it really quickly.

"But . . . Ugh. Jimmy."

I shake my head. "He's fine, Abby. I mean, he's still Jimmy, but he's really good on the drums. And playing with him . . . you kind of forget his Jimmy-ness. It's fun."

She looks off, like she's having one last moment of doubt.

"Abby! This is meant to be!" I get down on one knee and grab her hands. "Help me, Abby-Wan Kenobi. You're my only hope."

It's super cheesy, but that seals it.

The next day, Saturday, Abby and Frank meet for the first time in the proton center lobby before my treatment.

"You must be the world-famous Abby I've heard so much about." Frank throws a pizza-flavored Combo in his mouth and wipes his hand on his scrubs. Shakes her hand, bowing dramatically.

Abby looks him up and down. "You're hairier than I pictured."

"Thank you. I try." Frank puts the case he's carrying on the floor. He squats down and pops the latches. Pulls out a well-worn bass guitar.

"This old girl has seen better days." He hands it to Abby. "But she still sounds good. I dusted her off and got her all tuned up for you."

Abby slips the strap over her head. Tests the weight of it. She grabs the neck and plucks a couple of strings with her right thumb. Then she looks up at me with a big grin on her face.

"Oh, I could get used to this."

I'd called Frank, who said he could give her some lessons (he'd played bass guitar in a former band), but Abby texted her super genius (her words) viola teacher, Lisa, who said she could help her as well.

She agreed to try. She'd give it a week, and if she hated it or sucked at it or it messed up her viola playing in any way, she was out. But once she put that bass around her neck, I knew she was in. It suited her.

Again . . . like it was meant to be.

So, with exactly two weeks until the talent show, Abby goes after the bass guitar with the kind of dedication she usually reserves for her monster movie marathons. She basically locks herself into her room for the next couple of nights. She asks around in her music-geek Facebook groups and finds some online tutorials that she loves too.

When I text her each morning about how it's going, she gives me the same answer.

It's going. You'll see.

When I see her, though, the dented red fingertips on her left hand tell me the rest.

I go to my treatments every afternoon, then Jimmy

and I practice each evening (with only two near fights), and I play quietly in my room late at night. The calluses on the ends of my fingers are getting so tough they feel like rocks.

It's a Thursday when Sarah drops into her seat in front of me in Bayer's class. I haven't really said anything to her since the hair-pizza incident a while ago. I'm not sure why I find my voice today, but I do.

"Hey, Sarah."

She turns around. "Hi, Ross."

I clear my throat. "I . . . I just wanted to say I'm sorry again about the, um . . . pizza thing."

She flashes a quick, embarrassed smile. "It's okay, Ross. It just . . . happened. It wasn't your fault. It's fine."

I breathe a tiny bit easier.

"But I did notice you never came to any of the meetings after that. The planning meetings."

"Yeah." I sigh. "Sorry about that. I started working on something for the show, though!"

She turns around, giving me her full attention. "Yeah! I saw you signed up. What are you doing? Is it a surprise?"

I bob my head side to side. "Yeah. A surprise."

She nods for a few seconds. Morphs into Concern Face.

"How are you feeling? How's your eye?"

"It's okay."

"Is it . . . gonna be okay? Will it be the same, or . . ."

I'm not sure why, but I tell her the thing I haven't told anyone but Abby. "Well . . . I'm gonna lose the vision in it, eventually, but for now it just stings all the time."

Her face drops, and she pulls back ever so slightly for a second. I see a flash of "skeeved out" pass over her face, but she recovers quickly. "Whoa. Like . . . blind?"

I nod, and she goes on.

"In just that eye, or both?"

I don't love talking about this stuff, but I'm having a legit conversation with Sarah Kennedy! "Well . . . they hope it's just this eye. Like, almost definitely just this one, but they said time will tell."

She looks fascinated. "Wooooow. I'm really sorry, Ross. That's terrible."

Then it happens. She reaches out and puts her hand on mine. I know it's just a gesture, but my heart speeds up.

And right then, at that crucial moment, Ms. Bayer decides to start class. I groan inwardly as Sarah gives me a pat and turns away. I sit back and slowly pull my hand to myself. Let it rest in my lap like some kind of cherished relic.

Then I make the mistake of looking over at Jimmy, who's watching me with a big smirk on his face. He waggles his eyebrows, and I look away.

Still a jerk.

31

CHECKING IN

Frank strolls into the lobby that next Monday waving a piece of paper at me. It has an address scrawled on it.

"I got the address. You still up for going to see Jerry today?"

He had texted me and my dad late last night to tell me Jerry was back at home and would my parents let Frank take me to visit Jerry between my treatment and practice. They thought it was a great idea, and I was really excited to see the old guy.

So, after my treatment, I climb into the passenger seat of Frank's antique of a Jeep—after throwing some empty Gatorade bottles and fast-food trash in the back. He blasts Johnny Cash on the way over. Says a little Cash is good for the soul.

Jerry and his wife live about five minutes away, on Washington Street. Their neighborhood is full of smaller brick homes. Mostly older people. I think Abby's great-aunt lives over here somewhere.

When we pull up, there's a woman slowly raking leaves out front.

"There's Marilyn."

She waves and drops the rake. She's dressed in a sweater that seems too nice for yard work.

"Oh, you came! Jerry'll be so excited." She peels off her dirty gloves and gives us both a hug. She smells like my gammy. "Ross, I'm Marilyn. Jerry's told me all about you. Y'all come in."

She has a Southern accent I wasn't expecting.

We climb the green-carpeted front steps—it looks like Astroturf, actually—and she opens the front door.

"Jerry? Look alive, you have visitors."

We step into a wall of warmth—maybe it's extra warm because of his pneumonia—and Jerry is there in a big, overstuffed recliner. He has an oxygen tube in his nose, and right away I think he seems . . . smaller.

When Jerry sees us, he tries to look annoyed. "Aw, fer cryin' out loud. Can't a man get a moment of peace around here?" Then he laughs and his face lights up. "It's good to see you fellas!" His voice is even rougher and raspier than usual. But it's great to see him. Over his pajamas, he's wearing a white robe with Mountain Dew logos all over it.

"Good of you to dress up for us, Jerry." Frank stops and looks around the cozy living room. "But nice digs!"

There are framed photos everywhere. On tables, all over the walls. It looks like 90 percent of them are of their grandkids.

"Thank you, Frank. Nicest thing I've ever heard you say."

Marilyn is heading to the back of the house. "You boys want some sweet tea?"

We both say sure, but once she's in the kitchen, Jerry leans forward like he has a secret. "You might think twice. Marilyn's from Texas, originally. She puts so much sugar in her tea you could stand a spoon in it."

I nod. "Good to know. I'll be careful."

Jerry waves his hand at the room. "Grab a seat. Sit a spell. I'm not going anywhere."

I sit on the couch by him while Frank grabs a wooden chair from a small puzzle table. There's a half-finished jigsaw puzzle there—a picture of the Eiffel Tower and a bunch of flowers.

Jerry wipes his face with a handkerchief. "Marilyn said my favorite radiation tech might be stopping by, so I was expecting Callie."

Frank laughs. "Nice. Very nice, Jerry. She sends her love."

"Well, send mine back."

They trade barbs for a couple minutes as Marilyn brings in our tea. And Jerry wasn't kidding—I take a sip and my head almost explodes from the sweetness.

Jerry sees my reaction. "I warned you, didn't I? How are you doing, Dime Slot?"

"I'm okay. But tell us what's going on with you."

He quickly fills us in on his health. "Eh. The doctors keep saying they're gonna let me loose on the streets, but it's a trick. Three times they've said I was almost back to normal, then they pull the rug out from under me."

It's good to see him still making jokes. "Well, that sucks. What is it? I mean, what kind of sick are you?"

"Well . . . take your pick." He laughs and goes into

a short coughing jag. "Kind of a hodgepodge. Some pneumonia, some heart stuff. Plus the ball cancer. I'm a mess, frankly, but tell me about you. You've gotta be close to done with your treatments, right?"

"Nine more." I slide my hand up under my hat and rub my bald spot. It's become a habit. "Next Friday's my last one."

Jerry stops and takes a couple of long breaths. They sound difficult. Wheezy. "Attaboy. Good for you. I'm proud of you, Ross."

It chokes me up, him saying that. I'm not sure why.

Frank leans over and hits my knee. "Tell him! About the show next Friday."

So I tell Jerry all about the talent show. About the lessons with Frank and how I was gonna play alone but then Jimmy came along. And now Abby too.

Jerry looks like he thinks that's the best thing he's heard in a long time.

"Aw. Man. That is fantastic." He winks at me. "I always kinda wanted to be Miles Davis, y'know."

I ask who Miles Davis is, and it gives Jerry another (longer) coughing fit. "Frank, ya ignoramus. If you're gonna teach the kid about music, you needs to include some Miles, for God's sake."

Frank leans back and puts up his hands. "My bad. I'll take the heat on that. Merely an oversight."

We talk for another ten minutes or so before Jerry goes kind of quiet. His eyes look tired as he grabs a bottle of pills from the table beside him and pops one.

"Marilyn! I took a pink square one!"

She calls back from the other room, "Okay, I'll mark it down."

He gives us a comically disgusted look. "I'm sick of pills."

Then he tells us—in that blunt, friendly manner old people have—that he's wiped out and we'd better go.

"Oh!" I jump up. "I almost forgot. I brought you a couple of things." I reach into the bag and pull out the DVD set of all seven Harry Potter movies. "You said you'd seen a couple, but now you have time to watch 'em all. They're awesome."

Frank chimes in, rolling his eyes. "I'll back the kid up. They're pretty good. *Prisoner of Azkaban*'s the best."

Jerry takes the box set, looking amused. "I'll do that. I'll watch them. Anything's better than daytime TV."

Then I reach into my bag and pull out my sketchbook. The leather-bound one that was my mom's.

"I . . . I also did a drawing for you . . ."

Jerry looks at Frank. "He draws too?"

Frank shrugs. "News to me."

Jerry watches as I open the book and take out the drawing I carefully cut out earlier. "A true Renaissance Man, this one."

I hand it to him. It's a drawing of Louis Armstrong playing trumpet, from a photo I found on the internet. It's the first time I've ever shown someone one of my "real" sketches.

SKETCH
OF A
SKETCH

Jerry looks at the picture for a long time without saying anything. Rubs at his nose with one big finger.

"Thank you." His voice is extra rough, and maybe a little shaky. He clears his throat. "Ross. Thank you. This means a lot." He turns it around to show Frank.

Frank is impressed. "Dang, son. You *can* draw."

Jerry looks at it again for a bit before giving me a big grin. "Thank you. I'm gonna have Marilyn find a frame for this."

Frank launches back into ribbing mode. "That poor woman. Who do you think she is, your assistant?"

"Nobody asked you, Frank." He laughs. "Nobody asked you."

We start to go, but before we do, Jerry grabs my hand and wishes me luck at the talent show. Says he'll see me soon.

But I kind of wonder.

That night, Abby comes to practice at Frank's—along with both of our dads. Her parents were understandably concerned about her going over to some stranger's house, so the solution was that our dads would tag along.

Abby glances around as she steps into Frank's house. Sniffs the air. Frank has his hands on his hips, watching her.

"Does it meet your standards, Your Highness?"

She looks around a bit more before answering. "I've seen worse." Stares up at the crooked ceiling fan. "I think."

Denny and Jimmy show up just after us, and I watch Abby and her dad taking in Denny's whole enormous, tatted, long-haired appearance. But Denny's enthusiasm for what we're about to do wins them over.

"This is gonna be so rad!"

Jimmy, on the other hand, doesn't even raise his eyes when he shakes hands. Gives Abby a barely audible grunt of recognition. Charming as usual.

Finally, there's a knock at the door. Denny bounds over to let in Lisa, Abby's viola teacher. It's the first time I've seen her, and she looks like a librarian. She's not much older than Frank or Denny, but she's all proper and buttoned up. Her sweater is something Ms. Bayer would wear, and her hair's pulled back so tight it looks like it hurts.

Denny puts out an enormous hand. "You must be Lisa. Pleasure to meet you."

Lisa gives him a small, tight smile, and the contrast between the two is enough to make me laugh.

"Charmed."

Denny takes her jacket and introduces her to everyone. Offers her something to drink. She declines, but seems to relax a bit, assured that he has some manners.

When we head to the basement, our dads start to follow. I turn and look at mine. "Um . . ."

He looks at Frank and Denny, then back at me. "Oh. Are we not . . ."

Frank shrugs like it's up to me and Abby.

I feel weird shutting my dad out, but . . . "I dunno.

I thought it'd be cool if you saw us the first time at the show."

"Yeah! Sure!" My dad is backing up. "I get that. We'll just . . . Hang up here. Frank, do you have some cards?"

Frank walks over to a bookshelf and grabs a pack. Abby's dad looks at Denny, kind of excited. "This is great! Could I get a beer?"

Denny lights up like he'd been waiting for this. "Um, does a bear wear a funny hat?"

Abby's dad gives him a strange look.

"Yes." Frank chuckles. "That's Denny-speak for yes."

32

PUT A LITTLE
BASS IN IT

This probably won't come as a surprise, but Abby shows us how it's done.

She's learned the three songs we gave her and plays them like a pro. In just a few days! I mean, we haven't chosen complicated songs, but she's got these things DOWN. I guess knowing one stringed instrument helps with another or something? That or she's a wizard.

After a few fumbles, we make it all the way through the Eagles song. It feels amazing, and Frank jumps off his stool to give us a standing ovation. "That sounded great!"

"For an Eagles song." Denny has his huge arms crossed. "Can we move on to something else?"

Lisa looks over at Denny. "Not a fan?"

Denny lets out a long, pained sigh. "The Eagles are the dark lords of all things boring and beige and bland, and everything we should fight to destroy in this world."

A small grin slips over Lisa's face. "Well, aren't you charming?"

Denny shrugs his enormous shoulders.

"Listen." Frank holds his hands out to Denny in an I-get-it gesture. "There's a reason. I've done some thinking about this. Our objective here is to win a talent show, right? Not set the rock world on fire."

Denny just stares back, unimpressed.

"I know your views on the Eagles, Denny. I've heard them many times. But Ross and I've talked about it." He looks over at me.

I nod as he goes on.

"I like the harder stuff better too. But they wanna win this thing. And the Eagles are safe. 'Take It Easy' is a safe, well-known song. And teachers are the judges at this thing. Not kids."

Denny bobs his head, like that makes sense.

"And finally, it's simple enough that these guys can do it—a simple version of it at least—and sound pretty good." He looks around at us all. "Right?"

Everyone is nodding but Denny, until he finally tips his head back in defeat. "All right. Fine."

So we focus on "Take It Easy."

We figure out what to do instead of the guitar solo, which I'm years away from being able to play. Then we play it again and again and again, with suggestions from Frank and Denny and Lisa each time. And it starts to sound better. And better.

After our umpteenth time through, Denny throws a towel over to Jimmy, who's sweating like it's his job. And it's a job he's really, really good at.

"You're rushing, Jimmy."

Jimmy shakes his head while he wipes down his neck. "No, these jack-wagons are dragging."

"Seriously, Jimmy. *Please* don't make me play that song again. I beg of you. Just trust me that it's more of a slow roll than an up-tempo thing. It's called 'Take It Easy,' after all. So, y'know—take it easy."

"Okay, okay. Slow my roll. I gotcha."

I look over at Abby, and she raises her eyebrows, like, *Check him out!* It's weird to see Jimmy accept a critique without throwing something or stomping around like a mad little kid. He's really trying.

We practice for an hour and a half. And again the next night. And Sunday afternoon. Sometimes we run through other louder rock songs just to blow the cobwebs out, and to keep Denny from going out of his mind—those are some of my favorite times—but then we get back to the business at hand. And we keep sounding better.

It's pretty great.

33

SMEARS YOU CAN'T
WIPE AWAY

And just like that, it's the Tuesday before the talent show. When I wake up that morning, my bad eye has learned a new trick.

I'm in the bathroom brushing my teeth in the mirror before I notice that something's weird. My face looks screwy.

I close my good eye, and the edges of my face look . . . melty. Or warped. Like I'm looking at a wet painting that got smeared. Or like I'm looking at it through a rain-streaked window. I feel my heartbeat speed up.

I hold my toothbrush out in front of me, and it's all warped.

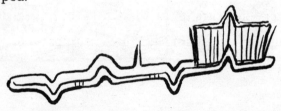

Whoa.

Something tightens in my chest as I walk into my room and look at a magazine cover with just my right eye. I can still see, but it's sort of like how things go gooey when your eyes well up with tears.

I knew the vision would go in that eye at some point, but I always assumed it would just fade away. Get darker slowly. I wasn't expecting the trippy, swirly thing. Or for it to get this bad overnight.

It pretty much freaks me out. It's kind of like having on glasses that are all smeary, only the smears are part of me. I can't wipe them away, and it makes me feel kind of like I can't breathe. I have to sit down on the edge of my bed for a few minutes and let myself chill out.

I mention it to my dad in the kitchen while he's pouring his coffee, and he makes a call to see if that's normal. He hears back from Throckton's office that it's unfortunately normal.

I look around at the cabinets. Out the back door at the yard. "It's a little like having a lava lamp for an eye, which isn't all bad, I guess."

My dad laughs, but at school—as I'm walking to my locker—it occurs to me that I'll never have normal vision in that eye again. My stomach drops, and I stop in my tracks.

I'll never have normal vision again.

I look around for a few seconds—at backpacks and lockers and the bright red GO BADGERS banner on the wall—until the panicked feeling in my stomach relaxes. A little.

All the same, I'm fascinated all morning by the weird ways my eye warps things. I can't stop looking around at stuff. At people.

Seventh grade! Now in WonkyVision!

It's freezing outside, so Abby and I are eating lunch at the table in the corner when Jimmy walks up with a bag lunch and a carton of chocolate milk.

"Scoot over. I'm sitting here."

I'm surprised, but I make some room. I instinctively look around the room to see people's reactions—this might be the first time anyone has seen Jimmy in the cafeteria. It's like seeing a bear sitting in a movie theater with a bucket of popcorn.

I spot Sarah and her friends—Denise and Angie—coming in the door. Sarah and Denise the Unpleasant are looking right at us. Or maybe just at Jimmy. Either way, I feel myself clench. I guess I'm now a known Jimmy associate.

Jimmy tears open his milk. "What's up?"

I look down at my sandwich. "Oh, just . . . eating, y'know?"

He takes an enormous bite of a bologna sandwich and nods his head aggressively. And I have to ask.

"This is weird, but . . . where do you normally eat? I don't think I've ever seen you at lunch."

Jimmy waves a thumb over his shoulder and talks with his mouth crammed full. "Down with Mr. Hanley."

"The janitor?" Abby stops with a grape halfway to her mouth.

Jimmy lowers his sandwich. "Is there something wrong with that, Princess?"

Abby unfreezes. "No! No, not at all. He's really nice. I just figured you hung out in the Grit Pit or something."

The Grit Pit is a wooded area just past the football field where some of the rougher kids hang out. You see smoke drifting out of there after school sometimes. It's to be avoided, if possible.

Jimmy gives her a look like she's lost her senses. "No. But thank you for assuming that." He takes another large bite. "Hanley is cool. We play cards."

I feel myself nodding, even though something about that makes me sad. "That's cool."

Jimmy gives me a look that's a little challenging. "It

is cool. Hanley's really smart. He gives me advice and stuff."

I hear someone's phone ding at the next table. Then another one, somewhere behind me.

"So." Jimmy takes a gulp of milk, leaving an impressive milk mustache. "You may be wondering why I'm here."

Abby and I nod. "Sure." Another phone bleeps farther down the table.

Jimmy's eyes change, and I see something that looks like . . . caring? Compassion?

"It's not good. It's really crappy, actually." Another phone goes off, and I look over to see a few people staring.

"I know who's making the memes."

I jerk my eyes back to Jimmy. "Who?"

Abby's phone chimes. She looks down at the screen. "Aw, man." She turns it over, and something in the way she does tells me it's about me.

"Is that another meme?" I ask Abby. "WHO?" I raise my voice at Jimmy.

I lunge forward and grab Abby's phone from her.

"Ross! Don't. It's just—"

On the screen is yet another Ross meme. Another cartoon that someone has changed.

The cartoon is of a blind guy—cane and all—about to walk into an open grave. They've put my school headshot over the cartoon guy's head and drawn dark sunglasses over my eyes.

Wait. Me . . . blind? The only people who knew I could lose my vision were me and Abby and . . .

I look around the room until I spot her.

Sarah.

She's two tables away. I catch her looking right at

me—and I just know. She looks away, quickly. My face goes cold as it sinks in, and I stand up without even realizing I'm doing it.

"Sarah?" It comes out quietly, but Jimmy and some tables near us hear me.

"Yeah. I overheard her. I was . . . Well, I was coming to warn you."

Abby's catching on. "Wait. Sarah KENNEDY? What the . . ."

I start to walk around the table, and Sarah gets up— like she's going to just stroll out, whistling like a guilty cartoon character. Then I find my voice.

"Sarah?" It's a lot louder this time, and the room goes quiet—except for a phone bleeping here and there as the meme spreads. "I told you about the whole vision thing in—that was between us."

She stops and turns to me now. The school is watching, so she doesn't really have a choice. She looks like *her* fight-or-flight response is kicking in. "Ross. I don't know what on earth you're—"

"Sarah made the memes." Jimmy states it, loud, cutting her off. "All of them." I feel Abby step up beside me, glaring daggers at Sarah.

Sarah takes a step back. "That is not true!" Her hand

drifts to her phone, sticking out of her pocket. Like a reflex.

"I *heard* you, Sarah!" Jimmy is still sitting, but he sounds disgusted. "You were right next to me at the lockers. Tell him!"

Sarah's eyes dart around, looking for her friends. "I . . . I didn't do all of them!" She blurts it out, and then looks surprised that it popped out of her mouth.

She looks around at the frozen lunchroom. "I did, like, one, okay? And not one of the bad ones!"

I feel my lunch threatening to come charging back up my throat. Like I just got punched in the guts. I can't stop watching Sarah. Her face is morphing into . . . something other than what I thought it was. And it has nothing to do with my screwed-up eye.

A girl two tables over—Janice Linder, maybe—yells out, "I know of two she did, at least."

Someone else yells, "Make that three."

Sarah's face goes from Flabbergasted Victim to Angry Demon in a tenth of a second as she spins.

"Whatever, Janice! You laughed just like everybody else! We were just goofing around." Her face morphs back to Sweet Innocent Sarah as she turns to face me. "Ross, I'm sorry. I did . . . Okay. I did two of them. Denise and I were just joking around, and it went too far. I'm sorry."

Denise lets out a loud (unpleasant) "Hey!" She glares up at Sarah. "*I'm* the one who only did two! Sarah really took to it."

Jimmy sighs, behind me. "I'm sorry, man. She did that new one today. She was telling her friends about it by my locker. I saw it over her shoulder."

My head is reeling. Me as a blind guy? Why did I tell her that? Was I showing off? What was I thinking?

I look back over at Sarah as Abby chimes in.

"Wow. What's wrong with you, Sarah?"

Then Sarah's just upset. Things are unraveling in her perfect world, and it's entirely her fault. I don't think her brain can compute the shift.

"Whatever, Abby! Since when are you guys all buddy-buddy with Jimmy, anyway?"

I look back as Jimmy picks up what's left of his sandwich and calmly takes a bite.

My heart is going like a snare drum. I want to start screaming, but I also want to go hide in a stall in the bathroom. It's like all of the emotions are having a four-way tug-of-war in my brain, and it's a standstill. So I just do nothing as Sarah goes on.

"So . . . what? Are you guys gonna run to the principal

now? Is that next? I can prove I only did . . ." She turns back at her friends, sounding cornered. "Denise started it!"

Denise, her face getting red, looks away.

I turn around and grab my tray as calmly as I can. Abby grabs hers, too, as Jimmy stands up. I'm starting to shake. I need to get out of here fast, so I don't have a public meltdown.

I walk past Sarah, looking straight ahead. She's clearly worried I'm going to report her.

"Ross. I'm sorry, Ross. Okay?" Something breaks in her voice, and she actually sounds like she means it.

I hear another voice—our vanished friend, Isaac Nalibotsky—yell from off to the side, "Unreal, Sarah. You must be really proud of yourself." I look over to see Isaac and his new friend Chris Stemmle coming over to us. "You too, Denise."

Isaac steps up and grabs my arm. "You okay, Ross?"

I meet his eyes and give him the quickest of nods. Somewhere in the back of my brain I register the gesture from my vanished friend—it's a sign that he's still in there somewhere—but I'm too much in shock to really absorb it. I nod again and keep moving.

I don't see this, but Jimmy tells me later that as Abby

passes her, she flicks a single Tater Tot at Sarah. It bounces off of her forehead.

Jimmy stops just long enough to look her in the eye. "Real classy."

I drop my lunch—tray and all, like the signs say not to—in the trash can and leave. We don't walk to the principal's office, but down the band hallway to the door we take to the loading dock. I sit down with my back against the cold glass. I'm having a hard time catching my breath. My eye is stinging, and my headache is back.

Abby drops down next to me. "So . . ."

Jimmy awkwardly lowers himself to the ground. "Sorry I did that in there, but I was just . . . mad."

I nod for a while. "Yeah. No. You . . . Thanks, Jimmy." I tip my head back and put in some drops. "I think."

Abby starts digging in her pack for chapstick. "See? I never trusted her! Nobody's that nice and sweet all the time. Had to be a mask, and wow . . . that mask slipped today, boy." She laughs—a laugh with no pleasure in it—

as she slathers her lips. Then she reaches over and rubs my shoulder. "Are you okay?"

I run my hands over my face. "No. I am definitely not okay."

I feel the hot sting of tears warming up at the back of my nose. I pinch my eyes shut trying to will them away.

"Everything is miles from okay. I can't . . ." I taper off, again fighting to keep the water out of my eyes and the shake out of my voice. "You know, on top of all this, my eye chose today to start going haywire too. Vision-wise."

Abby looks sad and confused. "Haywire?"

I let out a combo sigh/gasp loud enough they can probably hear it back in the cafeteria. "It's all screwed up and melty. Wavy. It's like it's starting to . . . I don't know. It's the start of losing it. Or maybe *I'm* losing it, or . . ."

Abby shifts over and puts her head against my shoulder. "I'm sorry, Ross."

"You should break somethin'." Jimmy looks as serious about this suggestion as I've ever seen him. "That's what I do. Makes me feel better."

Abby and I look at him for a bit. "Like what?"

He shrugs. "I dunno. A glass? A plate? I smashed the taillight out of a broken-down truck at my uncle's house, and it felt amazing."

"Yeah . . ." I put my head back. "Good suggestion, Jimmy, but I'll be okay."

He shrugs. "Suit yerself."

After a few minutes, Abby asks, "You gonna tell Principal Kingsley?"

I sigh. "I don't know. Maybe? I just need to think. My brain feels like a forest fire right now."

There's another pause before Jimmy chimes in. "So . . . the talent show is kind of Sarah's . . . thing. Are we still . . ."

My head snaps up. "Oh. Yeah. We're still playing, no question. And we're gonna win this thing. Right?"

They both nod enthusiastically, especially Abby. "Yeah, let's do it. What's the saying? 'Living well is the best revenge'? Something like that?"

I like that. "Yeah, well, let's do some serious 'living well.'"

Jimmy scratches at the elbow of his denim jacket.

"I like it, but hear me out. Slashing bicycle tires is pretty good revenge too."

I look over at him quickly, and he puts up a hand. "Kidding! Kidding!" He sniffs and looks away. "But you know . . . somethin' to keep in the back of your mind . . ."

34

MADSAD

As a seventh grader, I've never once thought about my blood pressure. But as the day goes on, I feel like mine is on the rise. Like I'm a cartoon thermometer, getting closer and closer to bursting.

A couple of kids stop me in the hall, individually, to tell me how much they thought what Sarah and Denise did sucked. They seem kind of ashamed, too, like maybe they shouldn't have seen them. Or maybe they laughed at them, I don't know.

I even get a text from Isaac.

Screw em. You okay?

I'm still angry with Isaac, and the fact that it's the first text from him in a couple of months just serves to make my mood worse. I don't text back.

My fuse continues to get shorter and shorter. I barely speak while Linda drives me to treatment, and when I get there, I'm a sullen mess. I sit in the waiting room hating the warpy-looking fish in their warpy-looking tanks.

Those dumb fish have never even heard of a meme.

Stupid fish.

I've just turned my wrath on the ugly turtle-looking carpet when Frank bursts through the electric doors, full of life.

"Ross, baby! How's it going?"

That's when I yell. It's just Frank and me in there. Throckton's office is empty, and I haven't seen the front desk lady, Susan. So I let loose with a roar. A long, loud one. Like it was coming up from my toes.

I don't yell a specific word or anything. It's just a weird, primal scream. Something a caveman might shout if a saber-tooth tiger stole his dinner.

"GGGYYAAAAAAAAARRAAHHHHHHHHHHHH!!"

Frank looks at me blankly until I run out of air. Then he nods.

"Gotcha."

I run a hand through my hair. "Sorry."

"No apology needed. But let's get back there before someone calls 911."

As we pass through the doors, Callie and an older nurse come running up. "Is everything okay? Did someone scream?"

For my treatment soundtrack, I ask Frank for an angry mix. He has just the thing. He pulls out a well-worn disc.

That day, Callie wears earplugs.

I lock in on my red X, although it's all smeary and weird-looking now.

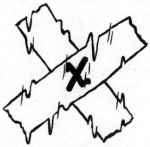

Too many things are filling my head.

DESPAIR: The girl I've had a crush on since fourth grade has turned out to be a jerk, and my best friend on earth is leaving in a few days. My only other real friend has moved on.

FRUSTRATION: My eye is making the world look weird, and it's messing with my head. I want my normal eye, and I know it's only going to get worse.

EMBARRASSMENT: That whole scene in the cafeteria was *brutal*. How humiliating and mind-twisting and . . . ugh. I can barely process the change in how differently I see Sarah now. After the years of worshipping the ground she walked on . . .

FATIGUE: The radiation has me so tired I feel like I could fall over asleep on the floor at any moment. And maybe not get back up.

PAIN: My head is throbbing. My eye hurts. It stings from the dryness, and the side of my face feels like a raw, gooey piece of bacon that might slide off my head.

ANGER: I want to light the world on fire and watch it burn.

That last one may sound harsh, but whatever.

Frank doesn't hold back with the volume. As the big mechanical arm starts moving, the music is crazy loud and fits my mood perfectly. Like Frank hooked my brain up to the boom box and my inner train wreck is spilling out of the speakers.

35

PLAYING WITH ANGRY

When I get home, I go to the basement and slam all the rage and self-pity straight into my guitar. At one point, I play what may be the angriest, least accurate version of "Sounds of Silence" ever.

After that, I move on to some of the harder-edged stuff that Frank has tabbed out for me. Rock stuff. Punk stuff I've been listening to on the mixes. I strum super aggressively and press the strings down so hard, it feels like my calluses might fall off. Part of me hopes they will.

It must sound terrible, or at least loud, because after a while my dad comes down the stairs. I see his feet and cool off a little. He sits about halfway down, and I stop. He's wearing his favorite Cardinals shirt, and it's seen better days.

"That sounded . . . therapeutic."

"Yeah. I guess. Kinda."

"Good. It's sounding a lot better, despite the . . . anger. You're getting better so fast, it's amazing. I might ask you to teach me." He comes down the rest of the way. "You okay?"

I look at the floor. My fingers are throbbing. "Honestly? I'm really sick of people asking me that."

He laughs. "Sorry. We mean well." He drops onto the couch beside me with a dad grunt. Gives my knee a dad pat. Turns and looks at me until I look back.

"Angry much?"

I nod and start strumming some random chords.

He settles back into the old couch. It used to be in our family room till the fabric got all pilled up. Now it's a basement couch.

"Ross. Have I ever told you about my boulder?"

"You have a boulder?"

"I do. You do now too." He looks up at the ceiling. "So, listen . . . you were pretty young. What do you remember about when Mom died?"

I stop playing. "I know she got really sick. And it was breast cancer." I look at the floor. "But most of it's stuff I've been told. I don't remember much. I wasn't even five."

He looks over. "Good. I mean that's good that you don't remember her being sick. It was awful."

We're both still for a long moment.

"So, here's how I think about it. The way I . . . visualize it." He holds his hands about two feet apart. "I was given a huge boulder that day. To carry around on my back. A big rock full of anger and grief and . . . all that stuff." He spreads his hands even farther. "Let's call it a three-hundred-pound boulder."

"That's a big boulder."

"Yeah. It is." He nods. "So, then—carrying around this three-hundred-pound boulder—I'm asked to get on with life. You know? Earn a living. Raise you. Make dinner. Be a good dad. Be a good lawyer. Get out of bed in the morning. Every morning! All while lugging this huge thing on my back. And it doesn't seem fair at all."

I'm nodding. "Yeah. I get that." And I do. I know my dad was sad and it was really hard on him, but I've never thought about it quite this way. How did he get through all that? And it's not like I was a big help. I was just a kid.

I notice a few new wrinkles under his eyes, and it hits me that he's earned them the hard way.

"I mean, everyone has a boulder, Ross. Don't get me wrong. But some are smaller. And I'm sure some are a lot bigger. But mine . . . mine got the best of me. Do you remember that?"

I don't. "No."

"Good." He sits up and leans forward. Elbows on knees. "But it did. It wore me down. It was too heavy. That's how I think of it." He takes a long, deep breath. "And I'm glad you don't remember that part. I was a mess. Drank too much. Slept too much. I could barely . . . Yeah."

He goes quiet for a minute, thinking about it.

"But do you know what happened then, Ross? After a couple of years of that?"

"You met Linda?"

He smiles. "I did. At the Hansons' barbecue. And—look—I know you've had your issues with her, but Linda saved me. Saved *us*. When she found me, I was nothing but a guy smashed under a boulder."

He takes a deep breath.

"She helped me shoulder that big rock, you know? She took that on." He reaches over and rubs my back. "She didn't get rid of it—you CAN'T get rid of these things—but she helped me with the *weight*."

We sit there for a while before I have to ask.

"So . . . why are you telling me this?"

He laughs. "'Cause I see you trying to carry your rock alone, and it's painful to watch."

"You want me to get a girlfriend? A Linda?"

This cracks him up. "No, you dork. Just . . . share the load! Release the burden a little! You can always talk with us. Or Abby. Or just yell. Just don't keep it bottled up."

I'm still confused. "But . . . I was literally just down here yelling."

He laughs. "I know. And I love it. I think I'm just trying to encourage you to keep at it."

Dads are weird. I nod.

"Look, son. Fathering is not an exact science. Maybe I should have just let you keep playing. Keep yelling, okay? Scream into the void. It lightens the load."

"I screamed into a waiting room today."

Dad pats me again as he stands up. "There you go." He puts his hands on the small of his back and stretches. "Good talk. Was this a good talk?"

I smile. "It was. Eight out of ten. Maybe an eight-point-three."

"I can accept that. You play. I'm gonna go do dad stuff."

I play for two more hours, until I can't feel the fingers on my left hand. Then I get on my phone and go down a YouTube rabbit hole watching videos of old punk bands. I start with the Ramones, but keep going. And going. I fall asleep to visions of Mohawks and smashed keyboards and thrash-dancing.

36

COURSE CORRECTION

I go to bed mad and wake up mad.

With a brand-new idea for the talent show.

The day flies by like a weird dream. That morning, Sarah—looking all sheepish—starts to come up to me in the hall, and I just shake my head and walk away.

In second period, I hear her get called down to the principal's office. Somebody must have talked. I have to admit I feel a rush of satisfaction. I mean, she deserves what she gets.

At lunch, I tell Abby and Jimmy my idea, and they're all in.

Frank and Denny like it too. Lisa needed a little convincing, but our excitement wins her over as well.

That night's practice has a whole different energy.

The next night's too.

37

THE LAST ZAP

Friday. December 19. That fateful day, to quote some song. A big day. Last day of school before break. My final treatment. The talent show. A lot of things have been building to this day.

All the same, it's hard to wake up. My eye hurts like there's a bunch of sand in there. But finally, I throw back the covers, swing my legs over, and sit on the edge of my bed for a while. Gathering steam.

I grab a shower, get dressed, apply stupid amounts of face goop, and adjust my Big Stupid Hat in the mirror.

I guess I'm as ready as I'm gonna get.

Abby is so jazzed up when she meets me outside the school, I think her head is going to spin off.

"Big day!"

We run into Jimmy in the hall, and he's maybe in

the best mood I've ever seen. He's wearing a new white undershirt (it still has creases in it) that he's written on in black Sharpie.

DRUMMER

"I figured it was time people knew."

The school day is both the slowest and fastest ever. At times I feel like the second hand on the clock has almost stopped, but the periods seem to zip by. My brain is everywhere but in school, and I may miss some of the finer points of Mr. Jarrett's American history wrap-up as I run through chord progressions in my head.

At lunch they play Christmas music over the intercom, and I realize I've barely noticed the season, I've been so busy and in my head. So weird. I mean, there are decorations everywhere, and I've barely paid attention.

Then it's final period. I'm not the only one fidgeting, as Christmas break is moments away, but I literally can't take my eyes off the clock.

My dad picks me up in the back parking lot and drives me over to the proton center, McDonald's fries and Cokes in the center console.

"Last one! You excited?"

"I am. But is it weird that I'm a little sad too? Like . . . I've gotten used to the whole treatment routine."

"Nah." My dad cranks the wheel as we pull out. "That just happens when things end. You've gotten to know those nurses and techs really well. And Frank, obviously."

"Yeah." My foot won't stop tapping. I have nervous energy for days. Plus, a healthy dose of angry energy. It's a potent mix. Better than Red Bull.

Frank is waiting in the lobby when I get there. "Ross! How you feeling, buddy? This is a big one. The big finale!"

I stop and look around the empty waiting room. I wish Jerry was sitting in his usual chair. "I don't know what I feel. I'm so nervous about tonight this all feels . . . weird. I feel weird."

Frank laughs. "Weird is good. We can handle weird. Let's do this thing."

Callie gives me a double high five when I get to the treatment room.

"Eight weeks! Piece of cake, right?"

I laugh. "If you say so."

The treatment is no different than the others, except I'm about to crawl out of my skin with nerves. I'm painfully aware of how many minutes there are until the talent show.

I wonder if I'll miss that big X.

Doubt it.

Afterward, Frank is out of the room, so Callie walks me down the empty hallway. She's telling me she's going to miss my face when the electric doors open, so I'm looking over at her and don't notice all the balloons at first.

Then I do. As well as the huge banner stretching between Throckton's office and the reception desk.

There's a small crowd. My dad, Linda, Abby, Frank. Not to mention the nurses, the receptionist, and Dr. Throckton. There are other radiation techs and business guys from the front office and a handful of people I don't even recognize. They all yell, "CONGRATS!" and applaud.

So . . . being the bowl full of awkward that I am, I

stand there, unsure what to do. I mean, I'm happy to be done, but I'm not really in a Woo-Hoo kind of mood.

Finally, Linda steps forward and gives me a hug.

"You did it, Ross! We're so proud of you!" I have to laugh as I feel her cold, wet Bucky's tea pressed against my back. And then my dad's there, too, and we're having a big gooey family hug in front of strangers. Yay!

When it's gone on long enough, Frank claps his hands a few times and steps forward.

"Okay, people. Enough of the sappy stuff." This gets a bigger laugh than it should. I think just 'cause people are feeling good. He goes on.

"Young Ross, we're all gathered here today for your graduation. I've zapped your head all that I'm allowed to by law, so you are officially done and *done*. You have my congratulations, as well." He steps up and shakes my hand in a really formal manner.

I give him an awkward smile. "Thanks?"

He looks around at the group of people, then at my dad, who nods. He goes on. "So . . ." He walks over quickly behind the reception desk. "We got you a couple of things. Well, that's not true. Your folks got 'em. They're just letting me do the honors."

He steps out holding the coolest-looking electric guitar I've ever seen. It's jet-black with a white pick guard, and it's love at first sight.

In his other hand is a small amp.

"Ta-DA!"

Eyes wide, I look over at my dad and Linda, who look like they're about to start bawling. Happiness, I suppose. Or some other parent emotion.

"Seriously?!" I step over and take the guitar, gently, from Frank. "This is the coolest thing ever! I don't . . . Wow! Thank you!"

"You deserve it." My dad's voice quivers, and there's a scary moment where I think he's gonna lose it in front of everybody. Linda, kind of behind him, has her arms wrapped around him and her chin on his shoulder. She's smiling from ear to ear.

I slip the strap over my head—it's black with skulls woven into it, so that might be Frank's or Denny's addition—and the guitar fits against my body like a long-lost puzzle piece. I look up at Frank.

"Tuned?"

He nods, and I play a few chords. It's not plugged in,

but it sounds amazing. Everyone around us has huge smiles plastered on their faces—maybe Dr. Throckton most of all.

"It's a used . . . wait . . . a Rickenbacker?" My dad looks to Frank as he says it. Frank nods. "Frank helped us decide what to get. Said it's 'choice.'"

"It's beautiful." I strum a few more times.

"Okay." Frank perks up. "One more." He walks behind the desk again. "This one's really less of a gift and more of a me-signing-the-lease-over-to-you thing. It's yours."

He pulls out the loaner guitar case that I could swear was sitting at home in my bedroom. He hands it over, and I can tell the guitar is in there.

I look at it for a few seconds before I look up at Frank. "Your guitar? The acoustic? You're letting me *have* it?"

He smiles. "Well, I mean, yeah. It's my cousin's guitar, originally, but he won't miss it."

I look down at the RiPE SPoNgE stencil on the case, and there's a lump in my throat the size of a Cape buffalo. I don't trust my voice, so I just point at the case with a questioning look.

Frank nods again. "Case and all."

Somehow the case means more than any of it, with its stickers from other bands and venues and its dents and scraped-away parts.

I'm not sure what'll croak out if I try to speak, so I just nod a few times. He gets it.

Then Abby is there, giving me a huge hug, careful of my hat and the new fantastically awesome electric guitar hanging off my neck.

"Way to go, Ross." She says it in my ear, and when I look up, I see Jimmy behind her, looking a little awkward. Somehow, I'd missed him. Abby and I break our hug, and she steps aside to let him through.

"Yeah, I came. Let's not get all weird about it."

He gives me a big, meaty handshake and punches me on the shoulder harder than he probably needs to. "Good for you for, y'know, living through this crap."

I laugh, and then Frank pops his hands together really loudly.

"Okay! As much as I would like this lovefest to continue, you guys have a talent show to rock in, like, no time at all, really. And you need to get your game faces on. Get ready to bring the thunder."

And just like that, all the nerves are back in a rush. My heart may even skip a beat as I remember we'll be onstage in a couple of hours.

Then Denny—where did he come from?—puts rock hands in the air and yells loud enough to scatter the nurses.

"TONIGHT WE ROCK BLOOMINGTON!"

38

SHOWTIME

Abby rides with us, and I thank my dad and Linda about a hundred times on the way to the house. I tell them we're going to need twenty minutes or so to mentally prepare for the show—and I mean it. There's so much flying around in my head it feels like a tornado in there. I can tell Abby's mind is buzzing too. Plus, we have some stuff to do.

An hour later I walk into the backstage area of the auditorium along with Abby, Jimmy, Lisa, and Frank. Denny gets a few looks as he brings in the drums and guitars. We find a spot for our stuff, and I duck up the side hallway to the lobby to use the bathroom. I'm so nervous, I've gone three times in the last hour. A bunch of kids and parents are in the lobby, making their way into the auditorium—the show is going to start pretty soon.

I'm walking down the side hallway to the stage door when I hear a familiar voice call out behind me.

"Hey! ROSS!"

I turn around and see Isaac and Chris Stemmle coming up the hall behind me. There are five or six other kids from my class behind them—Eric Jennings, Ellen Treacher—but Isaac seems to be leading them.

"Hey, Isaac." I look behind me, to see if anyone else is in the hall. "What's up?" I'm not exactly thrilled to see him.

He comes up and stops a few feet from me. He's wearing his huge green backpack.

"Ross?" He puts his hands out, like he's telling me to calm down. "Hear me out, okay?"

I nod.

"Ross. I don't expect you to forgive me for the way I've been acting, but I want to apologize."

I don't say anything, so he goes on. "There's no excuse. You're one of my best friends, and I've . . . I haven't been there for you."

He turns around and looks back at the others. He looks conflicted for a second, then drops his arms to his sides.

"Wait. I don't . . . I don't want to do this crap in front of you guys, so . . ." He turns around and gestures for me to wait again. "We'll get back to that. But some of us . . ."

He waves a hand at Chris and the others. They're nodding. "We got together and bought you something."

I look around at them. "You . . . got me something."

"Yeah. It was . . . What happened to you, with the phone things and . . ." This flustered not-finishing-a-sentence thing is pure Isaac. "We knew you were playing tonight, and . . ." He bends over and unzips his backpack. Then he pulls out a black cowboy hat.

"Look. If you don't want to wear it, just . . . It's for you. But you don't have to."

He turns the hat around and hands it to me. Someone has re-created one of my Batpig drawings on the front in white paint.

"Annie did the Batpig. She painted it from that one you did on my folder." Isaac's older sister is a junior in high school, and a really good artist.

"Thanks, everybody." I'm kind of at a loss for words, so I just stare at the hat for a bit. "Thank you."

Ellen Treacher is smiling. "Do you like it? I think it's kinda rad."

"I do." I'm nodding and looking at each one of them.

Another kid, Dave Dutton, comes running into the hall. "Did you give it to him yet?"

Isaac turns around. "Yeah. He likes it." He looks back at me. "All right, let me talk to Ross alone. Everybody out." He shoos them away. "You too, Chris."

When everyone is gone, Isaac turns back to me. Looks me in the eyes.

"I'm so sorry, Ross. I really am." He looks down at his empty backpack. "I mean, I'm an idiot."

I watch him for a few seconds. "What happened?"

"I freaked out, Ross! That's what happened. And I'm really, *really* not happy with myself about it."

I sniff. "So, you . . . freaked out."

"I did, Ross. When you told me you were sick, I just . . ." He puts his hands by his ears and mimics explosions coming out of them. "I had zero idea what to do. What to say to you. Zero."

I realize I'm nodding. "So you just didn't."

He looks up. Embarrassed. "Yeah. I guess. I'm not proud of it, but the whole sick thing sent me into a tailspin." He turns and looks up the hall behind him. "My parents almost made me go to counseling!" When he turns back, there are tears in his eyes. "But man, I miss you guys."

"But . . . Abby isn't sick. Why'd you avoid her?"

He lets out a snot-filled laugh as a tear spills over his eyelid. "Heh. But you guys are like a matched set. Like salt and pepper. Or peanut butter and jelly."

We stand there awkwardly for a couple of seconds. "Thanks for the hat, Isaac."

He wipes his eyes. "Yeah! Yeah. I mean, look. I wasn't expecting you to forgive me right away. I deserve more of a—"

"Seriously, Isaac. Thanks. I've gotta go. The show. But let's . . . You, me, and Abby."

He nods, and then starts digging into the front pocket of his jeans. "Yeah. Abby probably *really* hates me, so put in a good word." He darts a hand forward for me to shake. "Break a leg, Ross. Or whatever you say to a musician. And again . . . sorry."

I put my hand out and he gives it a quick shake, and he's four paces back down the hall before I realize what he slipped into my hand.

An Oreo.

I duck into the bathroom to try out the new hat, and Ellen is right. The new one looks pretty great.

When I walk backstage, Abby gives me a funny look and points at the new hat.

"From Isaac."

She looks at it for a few seconds. Nods. "Good for him." She keeps nodding. "He's still a jerk, but good for him."

When Denny's done getting things set, he gives us all high fives and says he'll be in the crowd. Tells us to break a leg, to rock the house, and to have a blast.

Then he turns to Lisa. "My lady? Would you care to join me?"

Lisa smiles and looks over at Abby, who nods at her. Lisa takes Abby by the shoulders. "You're going to be great."

They hug, and then Denny holds out one giant tattooed arm for Lisa. She hooks her tiny arm through his and puts a hand to her cheek.

"Well, be still my beating heart."

Interesting. Abby and I exchange a glance.

Then it's just the four of us.

There are a bunch of kids milling around backstage. Some are going over things on note cards, or have their eyes closed going through their acts. Pete Belford—a kid from my class—is juggling bowling pins in the back corner, and it's pretty impressive. I watch for a minute and only see him drop one.

He grimaces to himself. "Well, farts."

Frank steps over and puts his arm around my shoulders. "You good, big guy?"

My heart rate's been speeding up for the last five minutes, but I'm able to take a deep breath and blow it out. I tip my hat back and look up at him.

"Probably not."

He pats my chest and laughs. "There ya go. That's the spirit." Then he leans down just enough that he can whisper. "You've got this, Ross. Just let go. Go out there and just . . . let go."

I nod as he stands up. We fist bump, and then he does the same to Abby and Jimmy. "You guys are ready. Just go out there and do it, 'kay?"

We all nod, and he turns and ducks out the stage door, leaving the three of us alone. Or as alone as you can be backstage with a bazillion people.

Abby's broken out her best rock-star look tonight. She's wearing her favorite Vampire Weekend shirt, and she has her hair fluffed out extra big, with a swipe of dark red makeup going across her eyes.

She looks awesome.

She also looks nervous.

Jimmy looks like Jimmy, in his DRUMMER shirt and the usual denim jacket, but he's added a wool cap that gives him a vaguely rocker look.

I'm just wearing a white MUSIC IS LIFE shirt and jeans.

The crowd parts, and Sarah steps through with Denise, who's holding an official-looking clipboard. I think she's the stage manager or something.

Sarah is looking anywhere but at me—clearly embarrassed. I heard she and Denise got detention for, like, forever. I also heard she and Angie Moosebottom got in a huge fight over the whole cafeteria thing. Score one for Moosebottom!

I also heard the only reason Sarah and Denise are still running and hosting the show tonight is nobody else wanted to take over at the last minute.

A series of memes flash through my mind. Cancer Cowboy. The IV one. Death with my name. The one with me as a blind guy.

Principal Kingsley called my dad and told him about the whole meme situation. They agreed we should all get together to talk about it. And that—this part made my stomach drop—there might be a school-wide assembly on being compassionate.

Afterward, my dad gave me a big hug and asked if I was okay. We went for a long walk and talked about it, and I showed him the memes. It felt good to unload a bunch, and he mostly just listened. There were a couple more hugs and one ruffling of my hair. I felt better. Then, for the rest of the day he kept doing that dad thing where he'd try to look me straight in the eyes. Like he was checking to see if I was *reeeeally* okay.

"You're on last." Denise has an exaggeratedly extra-nice look on her face. It's obnoxious and overdone—on purpose. "Okeydoke?"

I give her a blank face. I'm not ready to brush this whole thing under the rug. "Sure, Denise."

"Great! Super." The added sugar in her voice grates on my nerves.

Jimmy is looking at her with real contempt. Like something he dragged in on his shoe. "Well, aren't you just the sweetest thing ever."

Denise turns to him, and every trace of a smile drops away. "Whatever. Did you know we got in-school suspension because of you turds?"

This makes Jimmy laugh out loud. A loud, obnoxious bark. "Because of us? You made the memes."

Sarah starts to walk away, but Denise grabs her arm

to stop her. Waving her hand dramatically in front of the three of us, Denise goes on.

"OOOH, we made a meeeeeme! Maybe you should all get over yourselves. It was a JOKE. Move on, freak squad."

I'm suddenly hot all over. Steaming. I look at Denise's pointy little face, and all I see is red. Sarah is stepping in trying to shut her up. Finally, they turn to go, but Denise gets in a shot, right at me.

"Do us a favor. Just sing your dumb song and then crawl back in your little hole, okay?"

I try to respond, but she slips away into the crowd. The words weren't coming to me anyway. I think I was just shocked that someone could be that much of a jerk in real life. Like, did she wake up one day and decide to be a bad guy?

Sarah gives me the weirdest smile I've ever seen. She reaches out and touches my arm. "I'm sorry, Ross. I did . . . I did those pictures, but I don't feel the way she does. I'm really sorry."

I stare back. Denise's words are echoing in my head, and I have too many emotions going to pick a facial expression.

Sarah looks at her watch and gives me an exaggerated I-have-to-go face. "Have a good show." Then she's gone.

I feel Abby's hand. She rests it on my chest. Looks me in the eye.

"Forget them. Shake it off."

I can't answer. Sarah's weak little apology did nothing. I know Denise is awful and I shouldn't let her get to me, but I feel like I want to ram my head through a wall.

I walk away to the loading dock door and step outside. It's freezing out—spitting sleet, actually—but it feels really, really good. I go to the edge of the platform and stand there taking in long, deep pulls of the night air. Watching the Christmas lights on the football fence twinkle in the cold rain.

A few minutes later, I hear Sarah's voice, amplified but muffled through the cracked door.

"Hello! Hello, everyone, and welcome to the big holiday talent show!"

Most of the show is a blur for me. I'm almost shaking I'm so . . . psychotic? *Psychotic* feels like the right word for what I'm feeling. I mean, I'm not going to start tearing the place apart like King Kong, but I'm WAY beyond angry. I spend a good bit of mental energy just getting myself to slow my breathing. To quiet all the things raging through my head.

Somebody juggles. Somebody dances. Charlotte Keenan

does a violin solo while riding a unicycle. Pete gets through both the bowling pins and some plate juggling without a glitch. But it's all like watching TV through a window. I barely register it. My mind just . . . spins.

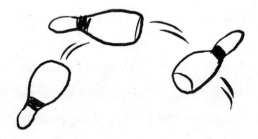

And then it's time.

39

CURTAINS

While some of the acts have performed in front of the curtain, we're set up behind the curtain because of the drum kit. So we're ready, in position and staring at the back of the curtain when we hear Sarah walk across the stage and take the microphone. I can feel my heartbeat against the guitar strap. I'm gripping Frank's trusty old blue electric guitar like my life depends on it.

"Thank you, Tiffany!" Sarah's voice is muffled a bit by the curtain. "What a great poem, am I right, folks? So great."

I look over at Abby. She smiles and reaches over for a fist bump. "We got this."

I pull out one of my little vials and quickly put in eye

drops, then flick the container into the Christmas tree over by the side of the stage.

Sarah goes on. "Okay! Now we have our final act of the evening. Um . . . please welcome Ross Maloy, Abby Peterson, and Jimmy Jenkins!"

There's applause and some shouting as the curtains part, and we see the audience. Actually, we *can't* see most of them, because the lights on us are so bright, but I'm pretty sure I hear Frank and my dad yelling the loudest.

I feel sweat break out over my entire body as I walk forward to the microphone. I try to adjust the height, but my fine motor skills aren't working all that well, so I decide it's good enough.

"Thank you."

I look out into that dark crowd, squinting into the lights.

The crowd is quiet, but my mind is anything but. I glance over at Sarah and Denise at the side of the stage. Denise the Unpleasant is giving me the most exaggeratedly bored look she can muster, and I feel my back teeth clench.

I turn to the mic and try to clear my head. I take a deep breath.

I hear someone clear their throat. I look over at Abby. She raises her eyebrows. *Come on . . .*

And right then, someone yells out from the dark. It's a deep, gravelly voice I haven't heard in a number of weeks.

"Go, Dime Slot!"

Jerry.

Jerry's in the audience? He made it?

Just hearing him out there sends a rush of warmth through me, and—I swear—it's like something shifts in my brain. Like that satisfying snap of a Lego popping into place.

It's a hard thing to explain, but a lot happens in a single instant. Maybe this was finally my epiphany. Just not the epiphany I'd been expecting.

Suddenly, everything but us playing this song seems beyond stupid.

It's like the part of me that worries about that stuff just fell out of my brain. Or like somebody found me the right glasses and I'm seeing things clearly for the first time in a long time.

I don't care what Sarah thinks. Or Denise. I don't care if we win the talent show. I don't care what people think of our performance. Or that my stupid squinty eye hurts. Or that the world out of my right eye is warping and changing by the day. Or about my big stupid hat.

That may sound like a bad thing, but it's not. It's

really not. It feels amazing. Like a nine-hundred-pound weight—or maybe a boulder?—has been lifted off of my shoulders.

I don't care.

And it's every bit as magical as that "every day is a precious gift" stuff other people talk about.

Blood flows back into my shoulders, and a smile slides across my face. I look over at Abby and smile. Then back at Jimmy. He nods.

I count us off, just like I did in practice a million times.

We start up "Take It Easy" by the Eagles, and part of me is picturing Denny out there squirming in his seat. But we sound good. Even better than I'd expected, because the auditorium has a pretty good sound system.

And then I'm singing. It's almost like someone else is doing it and I'm watching from deep inside my head, which is a weird feeling. I'm singing, and I don't even care how it sounds. This is for me. For us.

I sing a few lines before I look over at Abby, who's looking back, grinning from ear to ear.

And that's when I stop. I stop singing and strumming and turn around to Jimmy and Abby.

"Stop! Stop! This isn't . . ." They fumble to a stop, just like we practiced. They look confused, the way we did in rehearsal.

I turn back to the microphone, and you could hear a pin drop as the echoes of our music bounce around.

"That just . . . That just didn't feel right. Sorry about that."

That's when Jimmy starts in with a way faster, way harder beat on the drums, and Abby and I join in. I stomp on an effects pedal on the floor that Frank let me borrow. It makes the guitar instantly louder and . . . raunchier? Grungier? It sounds awesome.

Then I'm yell-singing. The song is "Judy Is a Punk," by the Ramones, and it's one of the fun ones. It's loud and fast, and it says what I want to say way better than any rolling country-rock song could. Not the lyrics—I'm not really sure what they mean. It's about the tone.

It's a song that makes you want to run and jump and

punch trees. It has that kind of energy, and it feels amazing to start screaming the lyrics. Abby's yelling along with me. Jimmy, too, though he isn't mic'd, but I can hear him back there.

It's sloppy. We know that, and we don't care. We aren't the Ramones. We're three dumb seventh graders, making the loudest noise we can, and it feels incredible. It's a song and a performance that will never win, and I couldn't be happier. I start screaming louder, my voice cracking.

When we get to the second verse, I reach up . . .

I pull off my hat, revealing my brand-new Mohawk. One strip of hair, right down the center of my head. There may be a reaction in the crowd, but once again . . . don't care.

So, I'd finally let Abby shave my head—*my* way, that is—during our "mental preparation time" at my house. I'm not sure I've ever seen her that excited.

I hadn't been going for a "moment," but Abby actually

got teary-eyed as my hair fell away onto the bathroom tile.

I look over, and Abby is still smiling big, but she has to concentrate—the bass part on the song is simple but it's super fast. I look back over at Denise, whose nose is scrunched up in a disgusted look—and it cracks me up so bad, I flub the next few words.

It isn't a long song, and as it's winding down, I try jumping around on the stage a bit. It goes okay until my leg knocks my guitar sideways and I lose my finger positions. But it doesn't matter. The song is just a loud, crazy mess at this point—just like I wanted. Like *we* wanted.

I start banging my hand on the strings, making weird out-of-tune sounds, and head to the amplifier. Just like Frank showed me, it starts squealing earsplitting feedback. I move back and forth, so the sound warps and wails like a stadium show.

The song ends at this point, but I keep playing with the feedback. Abby keeps making random sounds on the bass, Jimmy on the drums, screaming at the top of his lungs.

"YEAAAAHHHHHH!!!"

I fall down on my back and start scooting myself across the stage, banging the strings, facing the ceiling of the auditorium—until I bump into Abby, stumbling around the stage, strangling weird sounds out of the bass. This isn't music anymore, it's noise. Big noise.

That's when I jump up and take the guitar strap off of my neck and walk off the far side of the stage, between the curtains—but only for a second. I come back to the middle of the stage.

I look over at Jimmy, still bashing away randomly at his drums, and he gives me a smile.

And I smash the guitar.

I mean, I SMASH it.

I bring it down onto the stage in a big, long arc—as hard as I can. I put everything into it. All of it.

Anger. Frustration. Embarrassment. Stupidity. Confusion. Hat hate.

The noise it makes is nuts. Musical and destructive and eardrum-bursting. It's like an explosion of all the crap and bile that's been building up in me for months, and something lets loose inside me.

Out of the corner of my eye, I see Denise drop her clipboard.

Abby smacks a few more sounds out of her bass just as Jimmy stands up and kicks over his cymbals. They hit the ground with an insane crash, and he comes around to the front of the stage with us. Abby slips off her bass and lays it on the stage. Then all three of us walk to the mic and look out into the crowd, the squealing feedback dying off behind us. The crowd, from what we can see, is stone still. I lean into the mic and yell.

"*THANK YOU! WE'RE* COWBOY ROSS AND THE LOADING DOCK MISFITS!"

There's stunned silence for a couple of seconds until I hear Frank in the back yell out.

"ENCORE!"

Then the applause starts. And some cheering. Don't get me wrong, it's not everyone. It's maybe not like the standing ovation you'd expect at the end of a movie, but it's pretty good. Our families, and Frank and the gang, and ten or fifteen students jump up and start whooping at the top of their lungs. Isaac and Chris Stemmle run up to the front of the stage and start bowing to us like they're crazy fans, which is kind of awesome.

But there's a good part of the crowd that seems unsure *how* to react.

It doesn't matter. It wasn't for them. What matters is how I feel. How Abby and Jimmy feel. My body is still vibrating from all the volume as we walk offstage, and I've never felt better.

Then, maybe best of all, as we leave the stage, Sarah and Denise step back out of our way like we might be dangerous or something.

I love that part.

40

AFTERGLOW

As soon as we're offstage, Abby turns and pounces, somehow wrapping Jimmy and me up in one big hug.

"THAT WAS *THE* MOST AMAZING THING *EVER!*"

Jimmy is laughing, and I'm so happy I feel like my feet aren't touching the ground.

"YOU GUYS ARE THE BEST!" I turn and give Jimmy the most unlikely hug ever. "EVEN YOU, JIMMY!" He laughs and hugs back.

I faintly hear Sarah onstage saying "Okay! Yes. Well . . . wasn't that . . . something?" as we stumble out into the hallway beside the auditorium.

Frank, Denny, and Lisa are just rounding the corner as we come out. And Linda, my dad, and Abby's parents are right behind them.

"YOU GUYS!" Lisa looks more excited than any of us, which I did NOT expect from a viola instructor. Her tight ponytail has started to come loose.

Linda looks a little freaked out, frankly. "YOUR HAIR!" Not mad, just really surprised.

Then my dad comes up. "Did you just . . . Whose guitar was that?" He turns to Frank, who is laughing. "Did he just smash your guitar?"

Frank waves a thumb at my dad. "You'd better tell him, Ross."

So, I do, as Linda holds me at arm's length to inspect my Mohawk.

"I swapped it out. The guitar. Frank had another blue guitar that was busted 'cause Denny drove over it."

Denny tips his head and smiles, like he's either embarrassed or proud, I'm not sure. "That's true. I did."

I go on. "So, when I walked offstage, the busted one was there."

My dad has his hands on his hips, nodding. "Wow. Okay. Now about the hair . . ."

I shrug, and Abby—arm in arm with her parents—speaks up in my defense. "He was partly bald anyway, Mr. Maloy."

"Yeah. True." He's still nodding, and I wonder which way this is going to break. Then he smiles. "I think I like it." He reaches out and gives the strip of hair a rub.

I look at Jimmy, who's high-fiving with Denny, and realize his parents aren't there. He doesn't seem fazed by it, but I notice.

I turn to Frank. "Is Jerry here? That was him that yelled, right?" And just then, Jerry comes around the corner of the hall. He's in a wheelchair that Callie is pushing.

"Dime Slot!"

He raises one arm and pumps it as well as he can—with a rock hand.

This brings on some laughs from us, and some coughing from him.

"Jerry! I can't believe you came! That's so cool!"

He laughs as they roll up. "Wouldn't miss it. Whatever *it* was. Was that second thing supposed to be music?" But he's smiling.

I shake his hand and realize he's lost weight even since I saw him. But his grin is as big as the day I met him.

"Good for you, Ross. Good for you." He takes a slow, labored breath. "Not so good for that poor guitar, but good for you." Which gets a good laugh from us all.

We all eventually head back through the lobby into the auditorium—all except Callie and Jerry, who head out to get him some rest—to hear the judges' results. As we come in the door, Isaac is standing there like he's been waiting on us, a big goofy grin on his face. Chris is there, too, just behind him. Isaac's looking back and forth between Abby and me, and I realize there are tears in his eyes, a quivery smile on his lips.

"I want to be you guys when I grow up." He throws his arms around my neck and gives me a bear hug that almost knocks me off my feet. Then Abby. He's wiping his eyes when Abby finally talks to him.

"Okay. Come on, Dummy. And bring Chris."

We all file into the back row.

We don't win, but I don't care. It's pretty tough to beat a classical solo on a unicycle.

Afterward, someone suggests we should all go get food. There's some discussion about where to go before Jimmy pipes up.

"Does anybody like Dagwood's?"

41

ONWARD

Three days later, Abby and I are sitting on the front steps of her house, bundled up, looking at her dad's ridiculously overstuffed SUV. Every few minutes, her mom or dad runs in and out of the empty house, trying to figure out what to do with the full trash bags and cleaning bottles that are left.

The moving van pulled away twenty minutes ago with most of their stuff, and the rest is in the Honda Pilot at the curb.

"Is there room in there for you?"

Abby keeps rubbing her Converse together nervously. "Yeah. Between the cooler and the suitcases, there's about an eight-inch gap for me to cram myself into."

"Well, that's nice."

"Yep." She blows a loose orange curl out of her face.

"I think I'll be good so long as I suck in the whole way to Minnesota."

"Oh." I poke her. "With everything going on, I don't have a Christmas gift for you. I'll have to send one to you."

She smiles. "Yeah, I didn't get to that either. It's been . . . busy."

That's when both of her parents come out of the front door together. Her mom is holding her keys, a bottle of Fantastik cleaner, and a wad of used paper towels.

"And that's that. Abby? Any last words before we close her up?"

Abby turns and cups a mittened hand by her mouth. Yells.

"Bye, house! You've been a good one!"

Her dad takes the keys from her mom. "Well said. I couldn't have put it better." He shuts the door and locks both locks as Abby and I make our way to the sidewalk.

Her mom gives me a huge hug. "This isn't good-bye, Ross. Obviously. You can come visit anytime. Or vice versa, you know?"

I nod into her shoulder, careful not to knock my hat off.

Her dad puts his hand out. "Ross? You're a good egg. Stay that way, okay? Don't become a jerky teenager."

I shake his hand. "I'll do what I can."

"Good deal. We'll see you sometime soon, okay?" He heads to the car. "You guys take a moment. But not a long moment. It's freezing, and we need to get going." Then he and Mrs. Peterson get in the car.

Abby flops her mittens against the side of her jeans.

"So I guess this is it for now, huh?" Her voice is quivery.

"Yeah. But we'll text all the time. We'll call. It's not like the Dark Ages where I'd just never see you again." That Cape-buffalo-sized lump is in my throat again, and there's an ache in my stomach.

"Right. Yeah. So, let's not drag this out." She sniffs and wipes her eyes. Shakes it off. "Everything's good."

"If you say so."

We go in for a hug and stay there for a minute, her head on my shoulder. Her crazy hair in my face. And then she breaks it.

"All right. Text me later."

"I will."

She walks toward the car, but with a few steps to go, she stops. She turns and walks back to me quickly. She puts both mittened hands on my shoulders and looks me in the eye for a few long seconds.

"You're okay. You're gonna be okay."

I smile and nod.

She tips her head forward, eyebrows up, like she's making sure.

I nod again.

She pats my shoulder. "All right." Pats my cheek. "Okay."

Then she backs up as quickly as she came in. Turns back toward the car.

She opens the door and jumps in, and before the door closes, I hear her shout "Giddyup, people! What are we waiting on?"

Then her dad beeps the horn and they slowly pull away from the curb as I stand there.

It would be a great time for that sappy, final, waving-out-the-back-window shot if there wasn't so much stuff packed to the ceiling in the back of the car.

Then they turn onto Elm. And then they're gone.

I stand there for a while before I adjust my hat and start walking. It's really cold out, but walking home feels like the only right move today. So I do.

When I get home, my dad calls out from the kitchen, "You okay?"

"Not sure!" I head upstairs and into my room and close the door. Then I grab the acoustic out of the RiPE

SPoNgE case and sit on the edge of my bed. I'm running through some chords when my phone bleeps, telling me I have a text.

It's from a number I don't know, and there are a number of typos in the message.

It Jimmy. D gave me his old old phonee. Practice tmorrow, numb nuts?

I find a short video of a huge bear poking at a smartphone and send it.

You're on. Learn to type.

I pick the guitar back up and get to work.

I'm gonna master that F chord today if it kills me.

Oh, and life is a precious, wonderful gift from above. Cherish every blah blah blah.

My Dime Slot

Rob Harrell

In October of 2005, like Ross, I was diagnosed with a cancer right above my right eye, in the gland that provides tears. It was rare, aggressive and nearly unpronounceable: a mucoepidermoid carcinoma of the lacrimal gland.

A good deal of what happens to Ross in WINK came from my own experience. The biopsies, the surgeries, the initial plan to take my eye and blind me. The last minute reprieve by way of proton radiation.

The hat.

Fortunately, I was 37. Old enough that I could handle it. Kind of. I was living in Austin at the time, so a goofy straw cowboy hat didn't stick out *that* much. And I had my wife, Amber, to help me through it.

But it was an incredibly hard time.

I was writing and drawing a syndicated comic strip – Big Top. I threw myself into that as much as I could, coming up with daily jokes for a pack of circus animals. Humor helped me get through.

That – and music.

I remember the weeks after my surgery when I was laid up in a hotel in Indianapolis. My iPod was clutched in my hand the whole time.

I would lay in the back room listening to music all day long.

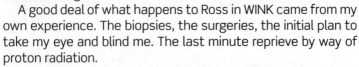

Music helped with the nausea and pain. It took me away, the way it does for Ross.

The recovery was painful, exhausting... and really kind of gross. I lost hair, and an eyebrow. I gained some scars – including *my* dime slot. Eventually I lost my sight in the affected eye. But laughing at myself, and the situation, has been the thing. The guiding light.

A few years ago, my best friend's daughter found out she had cancer. The tumor was in her femur, and they found it during a scan for a soccer injury. Her parents were there for her every step of the way, but she and I could talk about it a little differently. More candidly.

We only talked about it a few times, but I couldn't help reliving my own memories as I watched her handle it. Cancer is hard, but I saw how especially hard it was at that age. You're already wrapped up in daily drama – and then this?

WINK became the book I needed to write: it was a story for me, a story for my friend's daughter, and a story for any kid dealing with extraordinary hardships in life – and for the kids around them, as well. During my ordeal, I had Amber. But my friend's daughter struggled as friends peeled away, unsure how to act. Ross would struggle, too, but I was able to give him Abby.

For my friend's daughter, I was able – a few times – to be an adult who "got" the whole cancer thing. We could talk about scar care and how insanely sick you get of sleeping in one position after surgery and how sometimes you just want to scream. I felt like Ross might need an adult like this as well, and I was able to give him Frank.

And, of course, lots and lots of music.

At the time my tumor was diagnosed, it was the 25th of its kind ever reported. Ever. It was incredibly rare, but unfortunately the experience of dealing with cancer is all too common these days. It won't be an experience every kid faces themselves, thankfully, but they may "meet" cancer in someone close to them. Hopefully, WINK helps. And shows that with laughter and love and maybe some good tunes, you can keep going.

Thank you for reading.

While this book is a work of fiction, Ross' cancer and treatments were based on my experience with cancer back in 2006. The puffy eye, the surgery, the dime slot scar, the hair loss, staring at the big X, the eye goop, the vision loss: that all really happened. Even the dumb hat.

I don't think I can adequately thank those people who helped me get through it, but this is a start:

Eternal thanks to my doctors – Dr. Weaver, Dr. Shepler, Dr. Thornton, Dr. Sandbach, Dr. Kane, and Dr. Horn. I simply wouldn't be here without you.

Everyone at Midwest Proton Radiotherapy Institute: Thank you for making a weird, scary thing so much less so.

To my parents, my family, and friends. Thank you for letting me lean on you, and for sitting around watching the Winter Olympics in the hotel with us.

Thank you to the cartoonists who filled in for me when I was out, and everyone at Andrews McMeel Syndicate for the support.

Enormous thanks to my agent Dan Lazar, who helped me pull this book out of my brain, and everyone else at Writer's House for helping the book travel around the world. So many thanks as well to my editor Kate Harrison and to everyone at Dial Books who saw it as a story worth telling.

And Amber. Thank you, thank you, thank you. For being the best researcher/advocate/caregiver/partner I could have asked for.

In closing, if there's a caregiver in your life, drop everything and go give them a huge bear hug. Seriously. Go do it now before you forget.

Reading Group